80

**Other books by
Ann M. Martin**

Rachel Parker, Kindergarten Show-off
Eleven Kids, One Summer
Ma and Pa Dracula
Yours Turly, Shirley
Ten Kids, No Pets
Slam Book
Just a Summer Romance
Missing Since Monday
With You and Without You
Me and Katie (the Pest)
Stage Fright
Inside Out
Bummer Summer

BABY-SITTERS LITTLE SISTER series
THE BABY-SITTERS CLUB mysteries
THE BABY-SITTERS CLUB series

Dawn and the School Spirit War

Ann M. Martin

AN
APPLE
PAPERBACK

SCHOLASTIC INC.
New York Toronto London Auckland Sydney

For April Pezzaniti
and everyone in
New Market, Ontario
Canada

The author gratefully acknowledges
Suzanne Weyn
for her help in
preparing this manuscript.

Cover art by Hodges Soileau

ISBN 0-590-48228-9

12 11 10 9 8 7 6 5 4 3 2 1   5 6 7 8 9/9 0/0

Printed in the U.S.A.   40

First Scholastic printing, April 1995

CHAPTER 1

"Poor Logan." Mary Anne sighed as she stared out the rain-drenched window. She was already dressed for school and had come into my bedroom, although I was still running around trying to figure out what to wear.

"What's the matter with Logan?" I asked as I tossed a pair of baggy white cotton pants aside. The end of March was still too early for white cotton. At least here in Connecticut it was too early. Back in California it would probably have been fine.

Mary Anne turned from the window and pushed aside the bangs of her short brown hair. "Well, it's not just poor Logan, it's the entire Stoneybrook Middle School baseball team I feel sorry for. Look at this rain. Their practices have been canceled all week."

"Who cares," I said, stepping into a pair of jeans. "They haven't lost one game this season. Why do they even need to practice?"

1

Mary Anne looked at me, her brown eyes wide, as if I'd just said something shocking. "Dawn, the big game with Howard Township Middle School is next month!"

"So?" I shrugged.

"What do you mean, so?" Mary Anne cried. "That's the biggest game of the season! And this year — with the great SMS baseball record so far — it could mean we win the championship."

"We?"

"Yes! The Stoneybrook Middle School baseball team."

"Logan Clone Alert!" I teased in a ridiculous robot voice as I pulled my head through a blue hooded sweatshirt. "Logan Clone Alert!"

Mary Anne picked the pillow off my bed and threw it at me. "Stop that!"

Logan Bruno is Mary Anne's boyfriend. They're very close. But sometimes I kid Mary Anne that she's in danger of turning into Logan's clone — his twin. For example, Mary Anne doesn't care that much about sports, but since Logan is on the baseball team, Mary Anne cares passionately about what happens to the team.

Mary Anne's devotion to Logan's concerns can be cute sometimes. Other times it can be a little silly, even annoying.

I bent over and let the ends of my long

blonde hair touch the rug. Then I began brushing it. "I don't see why everyone gets so excited about a baseball game. It's just a game," I said.

I'm all for sports and physical fitness, but I honestly don't understand the competitive craziness that goes with it. If the idea is to exercise and have fun, who really cares who wins?

"If you'd lived here your whole life you'd know what a big deal the Howard Township game is," Mary Anne insisted. "They're our arch rivals. It was that way even when our parents went to school together. Every Stoneybrooker knows about Howard."

I decided to ignore Mary Anne's little dig about being a native *Stoneybrooker*. She'd never admit it, but I think she's still irked that I stayed in California for so long on my last visit. You see, I'm originally from southern California but my mom, my brother, and I came here to Stoneybrook, Connecticut, when my parents split up. My mother grew up in Stoneybrook and her parents (my grandparents) are still here.

Soon after I moved here, Mary Anne and I met at school and became friends. Then my mother started dating Mary Anne's father whom she'd dated back when they were in high school together. And finally my mother married Mary Anne's father, which is how Mary Anne and I became stepsisters.

Then, several months ago, I started missing my dad. Also Jeff, my brother, who'd returned to California to live with him. So I went back to visit for awhile. Mary Anne tried to be understanding about this, but I think it was hard for her. I think she felt I'd deserted her or something.

But now I'm back in Stoneybrook and glad to be here. Except, I'm in total clothing confusion. For most of this year I've been wearing lightweight, warm-weather clothing (which I *love*). Since I returned to Stoneybrook in December, I've had to dig up all this heavyweight clothing. But I didn't really want to put my lightweight stuff away because spring is coming. Only, spring is taking its good sweet time about getting here.

"Come on," said Mary Anne as she left my room. "We're going to be late."

I pulled on a pair of white high-tops, put on some hoop earrings, and was right behind her. Down in the living room, my mother and Richard (my stepfather) were already leaving for work. Well, it would be more accurate to say that Richard was standing by the door in his trenchcoat, holding his briefcase, while my mother searched for things she couldn't find. Mom is super disorganized.

"Morning, girls," she greeted Mary Anne and me as she ran a brush through her blonde hair while hopping on one foot. "Has either of you seen my other brown pump?"

We shook our heads.

"There it is," Mom said, reaching under the couch. "Now where did I put my purse?"

"It's on the table, Sharon. Please, come on," Richard urged her. He's super organized, but he's pretty patient with Mom most of the time. Mom's car was being repaired so he was driving her to work this morning.

When they were gone, Mary Anne and I went to the kitchen where Mary Anne toasted some sugary, jelly-filled cake thing that came in its own individually wrapped package. Yuck!

I had a bowl of raisin granola with goat's milk.

"Yuck!" Mary Anne said, looking over my shoulder.

"It's delicious. Want some?" I offered, knowing she wouldn't.

"No way," said Mary Anne as her breakfast tart popped up from the toaster.

"How can you eat that!?" we both said at the same time.

We looked at one another and burst out laughing. Mary Anne and I will never agree on food. My mother and I like to eat healthy

5

things and absolutely no red meat (which I think is double gross). Mary Anne and Richard eat a typical American diet loaded with fat, salt, sugar, and preservatives.

After eating, we put on our rain gear, grabbed umbrellas, and went out onto Burnt Hill Road. The driving rain had turned into a sort of icky, damp mist so at least we wouldn't get soaked on our way to school.

Our first stop on the way was to meet up with our friend Mallory Pike who lives on Slate Street. Unlike Mary Anne and I who are in eighth grade, Mal is only in sixth grade. Despite the age difference, we're friends with Mal because she's also a Baby-sitters Club member. What's the Baby-sitters Club (also known as the BSC)? It's a huge part of our lives. I'll tell you all about it later.

Mallory practically flew out the door, her reddish-brown curls flying. "Let me out of that nuthouse!" she said, rolling her blue eyes. Mal is the oldest of eight kids. Can you imagine? Things in her house are always hopping.

Next, we called for Claudia Kishi on Bradford Court. I smiled to myself when Claudia appeared. Her long black hair was tucked into a wide-brimmed purple rain hat with colorful Native American designs painted on the brim. She wore a matching purple slicker with identical designs along the hem. Even her umbrella matched! She is the only person I know who can manage to look totally fashionable on a disgusting, rainy day.

"What do you think?" Claudia asked when she noticed Mary Anne, Mallory, and me staring at her rain outfit. "I painted the designs myself. They're authentic. I got them from a book." Claudia is not only stylish, she's really creative and artistically talented. "This paint is supposed to be waterproof," she said glancing up at the gray sky. "I guess I'll find out today if that's really true."

"I guess you will," Mary Anne agreed.

When we had almost reached school we spotted Logan standing on a corner talking to Jessi Ramsey, one of our other friends from the BSC. Mal and Jessi are best friends, and Jessi is also in sixth grade. "Hey, have you guys heard the big news?" asked Jessi, her dark brown eyes lit with excitement.

"What?" I asked.

"The month of April is going to be School Spirit Month!"

Mary Anne smoothed away some rainy-day frizz that had begun curling Logan's blond bangs. "What's that?" she asked.

"I was just telling Jessi," said Logan with his slight southern accent that's left over from when he used to live in Kentucky. "My parents found out about it last night at the executive board PTO meeting. Each day in the month of April will have a different theme and event to boost school spirit. All sorts of cool things have been planned, like Clean Up Your School Day and Color Day."

"You mean we'll wear the school colors?" Claudia asked. (She was probably already trying to figure out how to work them into a cool new outfit.)

"I guess," said Logan. "The PTO thought it would get kids all fired up for the big game against Howard Township Middle School."

Mary Anne looked at me knowingly, as if Logan had just proved her right and me wrong about the importance of the game.

"It sounds great," said Jessi enthusiastically.

"Yeah, I guess," said Mallory, sounding doubtful. "Maybe. School spirit stuff makes me nervous."

"Why?" Jessi cried in disbelief.

"I don't know. School is there and some parts of it you like and some parts you don't. I don't see why you have to act like you're wild about everything. I mean, isn't that kind of phony?"

"Not to me," Jessi insisted. "I want SMS to be the best."

"And to beat Howard Township," Logan added quickly.

"Definitely," said Mary Anne, loyal as ever to Logan.

Logan looked at the sky. "I just hope this weather doesn't last too long. We have to be able to practice."

I kept quiet. But I sort of agreed with Mallory. To me, school spirit is the same as people going berserk over which team wins a sport. I didn't quite understand either one.

Sure, I like SMS and all. But did I have to jump up and down and yell about it?

Still, maybe School Spirit Month would be fun. I decided to wait and see.

CHAPTER 2

At 5:30 that afternoon, Mary Anne and I arrived at Claudia's house for our Monday BSC meeting. I promised to tell you all about the BSC, so here goes.

As I said, BSC stands for the Baby-sitters Club and that's what we are, baby-sitters. The idea for forming the club — which is really more like a small business — started with Kristy Thomas. One day she watched her mother try to find a baby-sitter for Kristy's little brother. Her mother was making calls all over the place. It occurred to Kristy that it would be a whole lot easier if her mother could call just one number and reach a bunch of baby-sitters at once.

Kristy told this idea to Mary Anne and then to Claudia. Claudia invited her new friend Stacey McGill to join them in starting a club that would meet three times a week to take calls from parents who needed sitters for their kids.

They put up fliers around Stoneybrook telling people about their new service. Meetings were held in Claudia's room since she has her own phone and a private number.

The phone started ringing right away. The response was awesome. It wasn't long before the girls needed another sitter to help handle all the job calls that were coming in. That's when Mary Anne invited me to join.

Everything went along great for awhile, but then Stacey's father got a job transfer. His company wanted him to move to New York City (which is where Stacey was from originally). So Stacey had to leave, and the members of the BSC had to find someone to replace her.

That's when Jessi and Mallory came in. Since they are younger they only work in the daytime. But that leaves the rest of us free to take on more night jobs, so it's a big help.

Pretty soon, though, Stacey came *back* to Stoneybrook. Sad to say, her parents had decided to get divorced while they were in New York, and Mrs. McGill returned to Stoneybrook with Stacey. We welcomed her right back into the BSC because we missed her of course, and because by then, there was *so* much work we needed her.

Then I went to California and Shannon Kilbourne took my place. She'd been working with us as an associate member, which meant she didn't have to come to meetings but she took extra jobs no one else could handle. But after I left, she started coming regularly to meetings. Our other associate member, Logan, remained an associate. Once in a while he comes to a meeting, but often not.

Now, I'm back in the club (obviously) but Stacey is out. Her leaving was really awful because she left on bad terms. She became super involved with her boyfriend, Robert, and his friends, and seemed less and less interested in her BSC duties and friendships. Finally, the situation blew up into a big argument, ending with Stacey quitting and Kristy firing her.

So, that's a brief history of the BSC. Here's how the club works. We meet between 5:30 and 6:00 every Monday, Wednesday, and Friday in Claudia's room. As I said, she has her own phone number, so we don't have to tie up anyone's family phone. Parents call us during our meetings. Whoever is closest to the phone answers any call that comes in, takes the information, then tells the client she'll call right back. Mary Anne takes out the club record book and checks to see who is free to handle the job. When that's decided, we call back the client and confirm the job.

All of us (except Mal and Jessi, because

they're younger) have official positions. Kristy is the president since the club was her idea. Also, she's very organized and always full of new ideas.

For example, the record book was her idea. Not only does it contain baby-sitting appointments, it holds everyone's other commitments such as Mal's orthodontist appointments, Jessi's dance lessons, Claudia's art classes, and so forth. That way, there's never a conflict in schedules. The book also contains information on our clients — names, phone numbers, allergies, special rules. It tells how much each client pays, and anything else we might need to know.

Another Kristy idea is the club notebook. After each of us completes a sitting job, we have to write about it in the notebook. Sometimes this is a pain, but it's very helpful. If you haven't sat for a particular family before, or not in a long while, you can just turn to the notebook and find out about the family. That way if some little kid is afraid of something such as, say, the toilet flushing, you know that before you even arrive at the house.

Yet another stroke of Kristy genius is Kid-Kits. They're boxes crammed with fun stuff for kids to do. Kid-Kits contain coloring books, storybooks, crayons, toys, glitter, face paints, stamps, stickers, and whatever else we can think of. (We're constantly restocking them with new, fun things.) We don't bring the Kid-Kits to every single job because we want them to be a surprise treat. But if one of us knows she's going into a difficult job (a sick kid, for instance, or one who doesn't want to be left with a sitter) they can be real life-savers.

Our vice-president is Claudia. She doesn't have any official duties, but we use her room and her phone for the meetings. She also supplies snacks. So it seems only fair she should be the vice-president.

Mary Anne is the club secretary. She does a *lot* of work. It isn't easy keeping that record book straight, and making sure everyone gets a fair turn, and scheduling the work at the right times, but she does a fantastic job.

Until recently, Stacey was our treasurer. That meant she collected our dues every week. No one likes paying up, but we need the money for several things. We help Claudia pay her phone bill. We pay Kristy's big brother, Charlie, to drive Kristy and Shannon to meetings. We pay for the stuff that goes into our Kid-Kits. And, if there's anything left over, we occasionally do something fun such as have a sleepover or a pizza party.

Stacey is a whiz in math, so she was the natural one for that job. While she was away the first time, I got stuck with the treasurer job. Now that she's out of the club, I'm the treasurer again and Shannon is the alternate officer.

As the alternate officer, Shannon fills in for anyone who can't make a meeting. Most of the time it's easy since no one misses meetings much. But when she's needed Shannon has to be ready to jump in.

I suppose I should tell you a little about each of the members. I'll start with Kristy. She's short with medium-length brown hair and brown eyes. She's very athletic and even coaches a kids' softball team called Kristy's Krushers. She's a sporty dresser who cares more about comfort than fashion. Some people might call Kristy bossy because, well . . . she is. She knows what she wants done and isn't shy about expressing herself. But I value her leadership qualities. Without Kristy's commitment and strictness the club wouldn't run half as well as it does. (Believe me. When I was in California I was part of a baby-sitting club called the We ♥ Kids Club. It was badly organized and I saw, firsthand, how crazy and mixed up things could get!)

Kristy used to live here on Bradford Court, across the street from Claudia, and next to Mary Anne. She has two older brothers, Charlie and Sam, and a younger brother, David Michael. Her father abandoned the family right after David Michael was born. (What a creep.) Kristy's mother was left to take care of and support the four kids by herself. Considering how hard that must have been, she did a great job of it. But then, something surprising happened to Kristy and her family.

Her mother married a millionaire.

No kidding!

She met this guy named Watson Brewer who is super rich. Kristy and her brothers moved across town with their mother to Watson's mansion in a very fancy part of Stoneybrook (which is why we now have to pay Charlie to drive her to Bradford Court).

It's a good thing Kristy's family moved into a big house, because her family grew right away. Watson has two kids from his first marriage, Karen (seven) and Andrew (four). They live every other month at Kristy's place. Kristy loves her new stepbrother and stepsister, and they feel the same about her.

The next one to join the Brewer-Thomas family was Emily Michelle who is two and a half. Watson and Kristy's mom adopted her from Vietnam.

Someone had to take care of Emily while Watson and Kristy's mom worked, so Kristy's grandmother, Nannie, came to live with them.

Kristy met Shannon in her new neighborhood. They became friends after Kristy's dog,

Louie, died. Shannon gave Kristy one of the Bernese mountain dog pups that her family breeds. David Michael named the dog Shannon, and from then on Kristy and Shannon were friends.

Shannon has thick, curly blonde hair, and large blue eyes. I wish I had her cheekbones. They're very high and interesting looking.

She has two younger sisters, Maria and Tiffany. The three of them go to Stoneybrook Day School, so we don't see them at SMS. I know Shannon is involved with a lot of after-school activities including the honors club.

Who should I tell you about next? Claudia! I've already told you about Claudia's great, unique style and her artistic talent. You should also know that Claudia is gorgeous. She has the silkiest black hair, beautiful skin, and wonderful almond-shaped eyes (she's Japanese-American).

Claudia has an older sister, Janine, who's an actual genius with some kind of amazing I.Q. Claudia is very different from Janine. Although she's smart, she's not interested in studying. She does just enough to get by and her grades show it. She's also a terrible speller.

I see Claudia's study habits and even her bad spelling as a slightly odd expression of her independence. She could get great grades. She could probably even spell, if she wanted to. But Claudia just wants to concentrate on art.

She's determined to do things her own way. Take junk food, for example. Claudia adores it. Her parents don't approve of it. (Neither would I if I were her parent.) So Claudia stashes bags of junk food all over her room. You never know when you're going to sit down on a bag of Doritos, or reach behind a pillow and pull out a pack of chocolate cupcakes.

Another thing Claudia hides are her Nancy Drew mysteries. Her parents don't think they're "intellectual" enough. (Now, there, I think they're going a little overboard.) But Claudia won't give up her junk food or her Nancy Drews. She's very much her own person.

I've told you about my stepsister and best friend, Mary Anne Spier. Let's see, is there anything I've left out? I suppose I should tell you that Mary Anne is on the shy side and sort of quiet. She's a great listener, though. And she's so sensitive that she cries easily when she hears about sad things.

Mary Anne's mother died when Mary Anne was a baby and she lived with her father, just the two of them, until Richard married Mom. He was overprotective of Mary Anne. He had all these strict rules and made Mary Anne wear really babyish clothing. But now that my mom's around, he's loosened up a lot.

The best thing that happened to me when I moved to Stoneybrook was meeting Mary Anne. She was very friendly. I liked her right away. She and I were the ones who got our parents together. We were looking through Mom's old yearbook one day, and we discovered that they used to be boyfriend and girlfriend. Mom went away to college in California and that's where she met my dad. (Later I found out that my grandparents sent her all the way to California to get her away from Richard, who they thought would never amount to anything. They were wrong. He became a successful lawyer.)

It took some doing, but finally Mary Anne and I got our parents together. And, as you know, they married. Mary Anne and Richard moved into our house on Burnt Hill Road.

Mary Anne liked the house. Who wouldn't? It's very cool. It was built in 1795. It's a little like a dollhouse with low, dark doorways, and narrow stairways. It has a huge brick fireplace and there's still an outhouse in the back (we don't use it, of course). The best thing about the house is that it has a secret passageway that leads from my bedroom to the barn out back. It used to be part of the Underground Railroad that helped slaves escape from the South to the North.

Mary Anne and I thought living in the same house would be like one endless sleepover party, but it wasn't. Everyone had to do some adjusting. Mom had to get used to Mary Anne's cat, Tigger, who she didn't like much at first. She also had to get used to Richard's orderliness. He had to get used to her messiness. Mary Anne and I started out sharing a room but discovered we got along better if we had our own rooms. And, we all had to get through mealtimes without being grossed out by what the person next to us was eating. (The smell of hamburgers cooking makes me want to gag, and Mary Anne says the sight of tofu makes her stomach turn.)

But, little by little, things have smoothed out and, most of the time, we're a pretty happy family.

Last, but definitely not least, are our junior members, Jessi and Mallory. Both of them are really sweet and very talented.

Jessi is a gifted ballerina. She takes ballet in Stamford, which is the closest city to Stoneybrook. She's already been in several professional productions.

To me, Jessi looks like a dancer. She's tall and graceful, with long legs. She has a pretty face with delicate features and, most of the time, wears her dark hair in a ponytail or bun like a dancer.

When Jessi's father was transferred to Stoneybrook by his company, the Ramseys moved into Stacey's old house. Their family consists of Jessi, her sister Becca (eight), and Squirt (almost two). Her aunt Cecelia lives with them and baby-sits while Jessi's parents work. Moving to Stoneybrook was difficult at first for the Ramseys because they're African-American and they were used to living in a very integrated neighborhood. Here in Stoneybrook most people are white. Some people were really cold, even mean, to the Ramseys because of their color. (That kind of ignorance makes me furious.) But Jessi and her family toughed it out, and now they have a lot of good friends in Stoneybrook.

Mallory's talent is writing stories. She wants to be an author and illustrator of children's books when she's an adult. One of her stories already won an award in school. She's also directed a performance of a play she wrote herself. It was about the hectic life in a house with seven other (younger) kids. It was based on her own life, and it was really good. These are the kids in her family: Mal (eleven), Adam, Jordan, and Byron (ten-year-old triplets), Vanessa (nine), Nicky (eight), Margo (seven), and Claire (five). They also have a bassett hound named Pow who used to belong to some kids we baby-sit for, Buddy, Suzi, and Marnie Barrett.

I think Mal is cute, but she doesn't. She hates her nose, her glasses, and her braces. (At least her braces are the clear kind.) She even hates her thick, reddish-brown hair, which she says has a mind of its own. It seems to me, though, that Mal has so much personality that when you look at her you see someone you like, so she looks good.

I feel as though I'm leaving someone out — and I am. Stacey. Even though she's not in the club anymore, I guess I should tell you about her. You already know some things (that she's from New York, and her parents broke up, and how she left the club). Stacey has permed blonde hair and blue eyes. She's pretty and, like Claudia, she's very into style. Like me, she eats a healthy diet, but that's because she has to. She's a diabetic, which means her body has trouble regulating the amount of sugar in her bloodstream. It's a serious illness. Stacey not only has to watch her diet, she has to give herself insulin injections every day. Stacey can be a lot of fun, but she got it into her head that we weren't "mature" enough for her. I wonder how she's doing with her new "mature" friends.

During that meeting, the phone rang pretty steadily. The last call was from Mrs. Barrett, who is now Mrs. DeWitt, since she recently married Franklin DeWitt, who has four kids of his own, Lindsey, Taylor, Madeleine, and Ryan.

"We need two sitters," Kristy reminded Mary Anne. One BSC rule is that two sitters are required for any job involving more than four kids.

Mary Anne looked through her record book. "Claudia, you're free. Want the job?"

"Sure," Claud agreed.

"Are you *sure*?" I teased. The Barrett kids could be a handful just by themselves. When you added the DeWitt kids it could be a zoo. Besides, the DeWitt kids and the Barrett kids didn't always get along.

"I'm sure," Claudia said with a smile. "I met Mrs. Barrett, or DeWitt, or whatever, in the Washington Mall yesterday. She told me things are a little crazy in the new house, but the kids are getting along much better."

"I think that when they joined forces to convince their parents not to move into that new house in Greenvale it brought them closer together," Jessi suggested.

"Mal, you're free, too," Mary Anne said. "Can you go with Claudia?"

"No problem," Mallory replied. "Lots of

bickering kids stuffed into one house — I'll feel right at home."

"That new house they moved to *is* kind of small, isn't it?" said Jessi.

"Way too small," Claudia confirmed. "But Mrs. DeWitt said that was the best one they could find that was affordable. The kids were so insistent on staying in Stoneybrook that they bought it."

I glanced at Claudia's digital clock and saw that it was after six. "Somebody better call Mrs. DeWitt back."

"All right, so Claudia and Mallory will take that job," Mary Anne said as she wrote their names in her record book.

"You girls are brave," I joked. "Very brave."

CHAPTER 3

At the end of homeroom the next morning Mr. Blake handed out a schedule of events for School Spirit Month. I sat at my desk and scanned the list.

Clean Up Your School Day sounded like a good idea. The recyclable soda can collection fund-raiser was good, too. There was even a Garden Day at the end of the month when students would get together and plant a garden at the back entrance of the school. All cool.

Then there were the less cool events — such as Pajama Day. That's right. We were supposed to come to school in our pajamas that day!

I don't even own pajamas! I usually wear a nightshirt or, if it's cold, sweats.

There was also a Dress Up Day. *Come in looking your best,* said the schedule. That didn't thrill me, either. I hate to dress up. I'd rather be comfortable.

Also on the list was something called Color Day which sounded pretty geeky to me. Each class would be assigned a color and you had to dress in only that color. What for? What did it prove? That you love your class?

I looked over at Mary Anne, who's in my homeroom. I wanted to see her reaction. I expected her to be enthusiastic (out of loyalty to Logan and the SMS baseball team), but I thought she might roll her eyes at some of it.

Instead, she was dead white. I'm not kidding! She looked as if she were going to faint. I couldn't get her attention because she was just staring at the events schedule.

I didn't know what to do. Luckily, the bell rang, signaling the end of homeroom, and I rushed over to Mary Anne. "What's wrong?" I asked.

Mary Anne looked up at me slowly as if I'd just roused her from some terrible nightmare. "This," she said, pointing down at the schedule.

She was pointing at Pajama Day. "Well, it is pretty dumb," I agreed.

"Dumb?" said Mary Anne, looking at me as if I were insane. "How can you call this dumb?"

I was confused. "Don't you think it's dumb?"

"It's more than dumb. It's a disaster. There is no way I'm showing up at school in my pajamas." (Mary Anne does own a pair or two.) "No way at all. We don't *have* to do this stuff, do we? I mean, they can't force us or fail us if we don't, can they?" As she spoke her voice was rising higher and higher, sounding almost hysterical.

I noticed Mr. Blake watching us. "Is something wrong?" he asked.

"Do we have to do this spirit stuff?" I asked.

"You want to support your school, don't you?" he replied.

"Sure, but some of this stuff looks kind of . . . dumb."

Mr. Blake smiled as he gathered his books and headed for the door. "Oh, you wait. You'll get into the swing of things once it all gets going," he said as he left.

I turned to Mary Anne. "I don't think Mr. Blake knew the answer to that question."

Mary Anne stood up and stuffed the schedule into her folder. "Well *I* know the answer. I'm not doing it and that's all there is to it."

"What about Retro Day when you come dressed as someone from another time?" I asked, looking down at my schedule and noticing the event.

"I'm not doing that either." Mary Anne ran

out the door without waiting for me.

I'd never seen Mary Anne so worked up about anything. Usually she's all for being agreeable and going along with official school things. Pajama Day had really upset her, though.

For the rest of the morning, I kept asking kids if they thought we *had* to do all the stuff on the list. Some said yes, some said no. Nobody really knew.

At lunchtime I headed across the cafeteria taking a sideways glance at Stacey sitting with Robert and her new friends. When she's not around, I miss her. But when I see her laughing as if she's forgotten about her old friends it really makes me mad.

At the far end of the cafeteria I took a seat with Claudia, Kristy, Mary Anne, and Logan. Mary Anne looked as though she'd calmed down somewhat. At least the color had returned to her cheeks.

"Are you all upset about Pajama Day, too?" Kristy asked me in her usual blunt way.

"No," I said as I unwrapped my cheese and tomato sandwich. "But I don't love the idea, either."

"Oh, come on," Kristy scoffed. "It'll be hysterical. It's one of the funniest things on the schedule."

"I have an idea for making a pajama set with the initials SMS silk-screened across the front," said Claudia.

"But aren't you supposed to wear your real pajamas?" Mary Anne asked.

"So I'll sleep in the outfit one night. That will make them real pajamas."

"I'm going to wear these pajamas Nannie bought me that are so weird looking I never actually sleep in them," Kristy said excitedly. "They have pink bunnies all over them. They'd be perfect."

"You *want* to look ridiculous?" Mary Anne asked incredulously.

"Sure, that's the fun of it."

"Kristy, you should wear your hair all stuck up on top of your head," Claudia suggested. "You know, like you just woke up."

"Good idea! But why just me? Why don't you wear your hair like that?"

"Claudia wants to look like she breezes out of bed in attractive silk-screened pajamas with her hair looking perfect," I teased.

"Exactly," Claudia said.

"This is going to be really cool," said Logan. "By the time the big game comes everyone is going to be wild."

Mary Anne smiled weakly. "I guess I could wear a robe over my pajamas." She thought about this a moment, then she shook her head. "No, I am not showing up for school in my robe. I'd die of embarrassment."

"Oh, lighten up, Mary Anne," said Kristy. "It will be fun."

I, myself, stood somewhere between Mary Anne and Kristy. I couldn't share Kristy's enthusiasm, but I wasn't filled with dread like Mary Anne. I'd decided to take Spirit Month one spirited day at a time.

That night, I went into Mary Anne's room and found her, still dressed, laying out her two sets of pajamas on the bed. One was a light pink flannel with ruffles. The other was white with red trim. Mary Anne studied them, frowning. "You'll be able to see my underwear right through both of these," she said grimly.

"So wear a leotard or something," I suggested.

"Do you think anyone would believe I sleep in my clothes?" she asked.

"Probably not."

Mary Anne sighed as she swept the pajamas off her bed and tossed them onto her desk. She threw herself down on her bed. "Well, I'm going to sleep in my clothing starting tonight and then it will be true," she said, folding her arms stubbornly.

"Don't worry about it so much, Mary Anne," I said. "You'll figure something out."

30

Mary Anne just rolled over, buried her head in her pillow, and groaned.

The next day was April first. Besides being April Fools' Day, it was the kickoff of School Spirit Month.

During homeroom, the assistant principal, Mr. Kingbridge, announced over the PA system that Spirit Month had been canceled due to lack of interest. Mary Anne smiled and sat forward happily in her desk. Then Mr. Kingbridge cried out, "April Fool!" and Mary Anne slumped back in her seat.

He went on to announce that the first Spirit Month event would be held during last period that afternoon. It was going to be a pep rally.

"A pep rally isn't too bad," I said to Mary Anne after homeroom.

"You once told me you thought pep rallies were totally stupid," Mary Anne reminded me.

"Well, I do," I admitted. To tell the truth, I don't see the point in getting everyone whipped up into a frenzy before a sports event. The kids in the stands are not going to be playing the game. "But even if it's stupid," I continued, "it's not embarrassing."

"That's true," Mary Anne agreed.

As pep rallies go, the one that afternoon was all right. The cheerleaders ran onto the baseball field and led a few cheers. (Cheerleading is another one of those activities I don't quite see the point in. In fact, I think it's sexist for girls to do nothing more than cheer for boys. But live and let live, I say.) The baseball team jogged out in front of the kids and threw the ball around. Everyone went wild cheering for them, since they'd had such a hot season. Mary Anne forgot her miserable mood and shouted, "Logan! Logan!" when the team jogged off the field again. Kristy put her fingers in her mouth and whistled loudly. Claudia waved her sweater around in circles over her head and shouted, "SMS is the best!"

"Is the entire month going to be like this?" asked Mal who was standing next to me with Jessi.

"I suppose," I said.

"This may be more pep than I can handle."

Jessi poked her on the arm. "Get in the spirit, Mal," she scolded with a smile. "This is fun!"

"Now we will all sing the SMS school song," announced one of the cheerleaders, a girl named Corrinne.

Everyone started singing. Even though I think the SMS school song is corny, I sang, too. Why not?

While I was singing I saw a blue van drive onto the school property. On the side of the van was printed *Stoneybrook News*, which is the name of the local newspaper. The van stopped and a man and woman got out. The man had a large camera with a long zoom lens around his neck. He hurried to the cheerleaders and began snapping pictures of them. He took some shots of the baseball team and of the kids singing. I noticed the woman talking to Mr. Kingbridge. She held a tape recorder in her hand.

I was impressed. The *Stoneybrook News* was covering School Spirit Month!

As the school song hit its final (almost unsingable) high notes, I felt an unexpected surge of pride in being a student at SMS. It was a pretty good school, really.

I guess I was feeling school spirit. Maybe School Spirit Month wasn't going to be so bad, after all.

CHAPTER 4

That Thursday the sun shone and there was a warm breeze. For the first time that year it really felt like spring. It was day two of School Spirit Month — Clean Up Your School Day.

The last two school periods were devoted to cleaning the school. Some kids policed the grounds, putting trash in big black garbage bags. Other kids raked the last remaining brown leaves from the grass. Some cleaned desks in empty classrooms, washed windows, scrubbed walls, and clapped erasers clean.

"This clean-up day is a good idea," Mary Anne conceded as she and I worked side by side polishing tables in the science lab.

"Definitely," I agreed. "The school will look a lot better after today. This is the kind of project I like. I mean, I understand the reason behind it so I don't mind doing it."

"What do you think the reason behind Pajama Day is?" Mary Anne asked, still polishing.

"Just to be silly, I guess. You know, to have fun."

"But it's not fun," Mary Anne protested.

"Well, maybe not to *us*, but Kristy and Claudia seemed to think it will be fun."

"Then let them do it," Mary Anne said sulkily.

"I wish Pajama Day would be over with so you wouldn't have to keep worrying about it," I said as I sprayed more wax on a table.

"I hope it never comes. Besides, after PJ Day there are a lot of other idiotic things I don't want to do. I don't want to come dressed like a student from another time. And then there's Backward Day."

It took us one full period to finish the lab tables. They really gleamed when we were done. Then we went outside and helped the kids picking up trash. It felt good to be outside on a beautiful day, knowing that normally we'd be stuck inside.

I can't believe what slobs the kids in my school are. I found endless candy wrappers, soda cans, looseleaf papers, faded folders, and old school notices on the ground. Some of it had blown behind bushes or against the building. "We should have a No Littering Day," I commented as I stuffed a torn, faded comic book in my trash bag.

"I think some of it blows off the top of the Dumpsters," said Mary Anne, looking at the large garbage Dumpsters by the parking lot.

That made me feel better. I hated the idea that the kids at SMS were so thoughtless. I always think of people my age as being more ecological than older people. So, if SMS students were this bad, the earth was in trouble.

"Even so, a lot more of this stuff should be going to the recycling center," I commented.

We made our way around to the front of the school. "Hi, guys!" Mallory called from a second-story window.

I looked up and saw Mal and Jessi washing windows. Mary Anne and I waved up to them.

At the front steps, Claudia was working with a small brush, touching up nicks in the blue trim on the front door. "Hi." She smiled as she carefully dabbed matching blue paint into the scratches. "Mr. Wong in the art department gave me this paint and asked me to do this job. It's not exactly thrilling work, but I'd like to head a mural painting team on Mural Day so I want to be on Mr. Wong's good side."

"What's Kristy doing?" Mary Anne asked.

"She's leading a squad of kids around the school hunting down any writing on desks, doors, or walls. They're armed with wash rags, erasers, and white paint. By the end of today, SMS will be graffiti-free," Claudia reported.

"Amazing," I said sincerely.

The time went quickly. Before I knew it, the final bell was ringing. I stepped back and looked at the school with its clean, raked grounds and sparkling windows. It really did make me feel proud.

On the way home from school that day I thought Mary Anne was feeling better about things.

That night, though, after supper, I found her sitting in her room with the schedule of events on her lap. And she was crying! Real tears!

"Mary Anne," I exclaimed, kneeling on the rug beside her chair. "What's the matter?"

"I can't go through with this pajama thing," she said, wiping her eyes. "But I don't want Logan to think I don't have school spirit. He's *so* into School Spirit Month. I feel like I'm being disloyal to him by not wanting to do this."

"Mary Anne, you're the most loyal person I've ever met," I said honestly. "Logan would never think that."

"Maybe not, but he'll be disappointed in me, even if he doesn't say so," Mary Anne insisted. "And all the other kids will think I'm a wimp."

"What do you care?"

"Well, I do care what Claudia, Kristy, Mallory, and Jessi think."

"Don't worry about Mal," I said. "I don't think Pajama Day is her kind of thing, either."

"Maybe not, but the others will think I have no sense of humor." Mary Anne blinked back more tears. "Are you going to wear your pajamas?"

"I don't know," I admitted. "I haven't been thinking about it like you have. I don't really want to wear them, though."

"Then don't," said Mary Anne.

I thought about it a moment, and the more I thought the less I wanted to do it.

Just then, Mom appeared in Mary Anne's open doorway. "Everything okay?" she asked. She could see Mary Anne's swollen eyes and my serious expression.

"Not exactly," I admitted. "We could use an opinion."

"All right," said Mom, sitting on the edge of Mary Anne's bed. "What's up?"

We told her about School Spirit Month in general and the dreaded PJ Day in particular. "I don't think you should be forced to participate if you don't want to," Mom said. "It's not something that affects your schoolwork."

"That's what I say!" Mary Anne cried. "But

everyone seems expected to join in on everything."

"Expected by whom?" Mom asked.

Mary Anne and I looked to one another for the answer. "By the other kids, I guess," I said.

"If the two of you feel as you do, I'll bet there are other students who feel the same way."

There had to be others! As soon as she said it, it seemed obvious.

"I think if you girls stand up for yourselves, and say you don't want Pajama Day, other kids will support you," said Mom.

"But what about the kids who *do* want it?" said Mary Anne. "Won't they be mad at us?"

Mom got off the bed and stood by the door. "When you do what you think is right, there are often people who get angry with you. You can't go through life worrying about that."

"What *exactly* do you think we should do?" Mary Anne pressed.

"You could ignore Pajama Day. Just wear regular clothes that day. Realistically, what could happen if you did?"

"Some people might be annoyed, but we probably wouldn't get into trouble," Mary Anne answered.

"So, there you are," said Mom. "Nothing really awful would happen."

"You're right," said Mary Anne, her eyes brightening a little.

"Thanks, Mom," I said.

"I hope I've helped," she said with a smile as she left the room.

"Did she?" I asked Mary Anne.

"What?"

"Help. Did she help?"

"Yes. I think so," said Mary Anne. "When the day comes, I'll tell Logan I forgot."

I scowled at her. "We're standing up for ourselves, not wimping out with lies. Remember?"

"Okay, okay. I'll say I simply didn't want to do it," Mary Anne said, jutting her chin out in a determined way. Then she looked at me hopefully. "Does this mean you're not going to do it, either?"

"No, I'm not," I said firmly. "It's too goofy and embarrassing."

"Good," Mary Anne said, her tear-stained face melting into a beaming smile. "I feel much better."

CHAPTER 5

Thursday

It's tru that the Barett and De Witt kids half groan close. They half no other choyse. The hous they life in has forsed them togither. In fact, you cud say they are even smushed togither.

Smooshed (I think that's what you mean, Claud) is not even the word. Crushed, crammed, jammed, packed is more like it. I'll never complain about my house again! (At least not for a while, anyway.)

On Thursday afternoon Claudia met Mallory on the corner of Slate Street and they arrived together at the Barrett-DeWitt house to baby-sit. They kept a sharp eye on the house numbers since they hadn't been to the new house before. "That's it," said Mal, checking the address she'd written on a piece of paper.

Mrs. DeWitt answered the door, looking super frazzled. Her hair wasn't brushed, she had no makeup on, she was barefoot, and she was dressed in jeans and an oversized blue sweat shirt. Claudia and Mal were shocked. Usually, Mrs. DeWitt (who is gorgeous with bouncy brown hair and a great figure and face) is turned out like a fashion model.

"Hi, girls," she greeted them. "I'm running just a little behind schedule today. Come on in."

Claudia and Mallory stepped into the toy-strewn living room and exchanged quick glances. The place was a mess. When the members of the BSC first started sitting for Mrs. DeWitt, her house was a disaster area and she was completely disorganized (even worse than *my* mother). She was always changing plans at the last minute, and never leaving the number where she could be reached. She was just divorced at that time and I guess it was hard on her. After awhile, though, she got her act together. She cleaned up her house and put some organization into the kids' lives. Everything was fine for awhile.

Then she married Franklin and their families merged.

Now it looked as if she were back to her old, messy, disorganized self. Only worse. Now she looked messy and disorganized, too.

Mrs. DeWitt must have noticed Mallory's and Claudia's expressions and she knew what they were thinking. "Living with seven kids takes some getting used to," she said with a nervous laugh.

"We have eight kids and we haven't gotten used to it yet," Mallory joked to make Mrs. DeWitt feel better.

Mrs. DeWitt didn't get the joke. She turned pale. "You've *never* gotten used to it?"

"Just kidding," said Mallory.

Mrs. DeWitt gave an embarrassed smile. "Oh, of course. You'll have to excuse me, I'm just a little rattled. I'm late to meet Franklin at his office and the kids have been just . . . well, kids." Mrs. DeWitt lightly kicked a stuffed tiger out of her way as she headed for the stairs. "Could you just keep an eye on the kids while I get ready? Thanks."

She disappeared up the stairs while Claudia looked around for the kids. A crash and the sound of shouting sent Claud and Mal running into the kitchen. "Where are they?" asked Mallory, looking around the empty kitchen.

Claudia pulled aside the sliding glass door that opened out onto a narrow wooden deck. She stepped outside and checked the small, fenced-in yard. There was no one out there.

"I've found them! Down here," Mallory called to her.

When Claudia stepped back inside, she saw Mal heading down some steps. Claudia followed her down the narrow stairs. At the bottom was a low-ceilinged, paneled basement with two twin beds. "This is our new room." Buddy Barrett, who is eight, greeted them excitedly. His thin arms and legs wiggled in the air as he jumped up and down on his bed.

His new stepbrother, Taylor DeWitt, six, was busy trying to do a headstand on his bed. "Are my legs straight?" he asked as he toppled forward.

"No," Buddy answered, then burst out laughing. He bounced two more times then flopped down on his stomach. "We got bunk beds first, but the top one came practically all the way to the ceiling and I banged my head whenever I sat up."

"What fell just now?" Claudia asked.

"Oh, that stuff over there," said Taylor, pointing to a pile of games that had obviously once been stacked but were now in a jumble on the floor.

"My ball bounced off the top of the pile and everything went down," Buddy explained.

"Well, we'd better pick this stuff up or all the game pieces will be lost," said Claudia. As she stooped to start picking up stray dice, cards, and play money, Claudia realized the other Barrett-DeWitt kids were still on the loose and might be driving Mrs. DeWitt crazy as she attempted to get ready. "Mal, why don't you see if you can find the others," she suggested. "Bring them down here."

"Okay," Mallory agreed, heading up the stairs.

Buddy and Taylor helped Claudia pick up the game pieces. "Those girls can't come down here. This is boy land," said Buddy.

Claudia looked around at the sports posters and pennants on the wall. There were footballs, action figures, baseballs, bats, mitts, and helmets everywhere. It sure did look like "boy land."

"Ryan's a boy," Claudia reminded him.

"No babies, either," said Taylor, "even boy babies."

Claudia stuffed a wad of green money into a Monopoly game. "Come on, guys, don't be that way."

"All right, they can come down, just for today," Buddy gave in.

Mallory soon returned with Suzi (five), Madeleine (four), and Lindsey (eight). Lindsey carried Ryan, who is two, and Mallory carried Marnie who is almost two.

"Hey, Lindsey, watch this!" cried Buddy. He bounced hard on the bed then threw himself forward into a flip, landing flat on his back.

"Bet you can't do this," said Lindsey as she set Ryan on the floor. She sprang into a neat cartwheel, but crashed into Ryan's red wagon that was crammed full of Power Ranger, X-Men, and G.I. Joe figures. "Ow! Ow!" she cried, clutching her foot.

"Ryan, no!" Mallory exclaimed. She leaped across the room in time to stop him from putting a red peg from one of the games into his mouth.

"This place is a disaster area," said Claudia as she rubbed Lindsey's ankle. "Let's all go upstairs."

The kids, Mallory, and Claudia trooped upstairs to the living room just as Mrs. DeWitt was coming down. Claudia was glad to see her looking like her regular gorgeous self with her hair swept into a French twist, her makeup on, and wearing a black velvet pants suit with gold jewelry. She carefully picked her way through the toys on the floor.

"Franklin and I will be at the cineplex catching a matinee," she told Claudia and Mallory. Mrs. DeWitt fished in her purse and brought up a handful of dollars. "Here," she said, stuffing the money into Claudia's hands. "Call for pizza for supper."

"All right," said Claudia.

Mrs. DeWitt pulled on her jacket and headed for the door. "Be good, kids," she called, blowing a general kiss to all of them.

Claudia told me Mrs. DeWitt hurried out so fast that Claud had the feeling she was fleeing the house, almost running to get out of there.

Claudia looked around the place and frowned. She isn't a neat freak or anything, but she couldn't stand to spend the rest of the evening tripping over everything.

"I know," said Claudia brightly. "Why don't we pick all this stuff up and then we can have some room to play in."

"We can't pick it up," Suzi protested.

"Why not?" asked Mallory.

"There's no place to put it."

"We'll find places," Claudia said optimistically. "We'll start by making piles. Everything that belongs in Lindsey's room will go on the couch. Everything that belongs in Suzi's room will go over here."

"Suzi, Madeleine, and I share a room," said Lindsey.

"All right, then we'll put all the big-girl stuff together," Claudia said.

"I'm a big girl!" Madeleine cried, happy to be included in that group.

Claudia ruffled Madeleine's dark hair affectionately. "The stuff that belongs in Ryan's room will — "

"Ryan doesn't have a room," Taylor spoke up.

"Why not?" Mal asked, puzzled.

"He was supposed to sleep in the room with Marnie, but she still wakes up in the night and then she wakes up Ryan and between the two of them our parents are up all night, so they moved Ryan's crib into the hallway," said Lindsey. "I guess you could say the hallway is his room."

"All right, then," said Claudia. "Ryan's hallway stuff will go over here."

It took about an hour, but finally there were five big piles in the living room. Buddy and Taylor began taking their things down to the basement. Mallory and Claudia helped Suzi, Madeleine, and Lindsey carry their things upstairs. Halfway there, the bulging Barbie case Suzi was carrying burst open, sending about seven Barbies and their clothes and tiny plastic accessories rolling down the stairs. "We'll come back for that later," said Mallory as she stood behind Ryan and Marnie who were working hard to climb the stairs.

"Don't let them eat those Barbie shoes," Claudia warned her.

On the second floor, the girls came to Ryan's crib in the narrow hallway. Lined up behind the crib were four unmatched dressers. "Whose are these?" Claudia asked.

"Ryan's, Lindsey's, and Mom's and Franklin's," Suzi said.

Claudia couldn't believe that Mr. and Mrs. DeWitt had a room so small that even dressers didn't fit in.

They squeezed past the crib and dressers and into the room the girls shared. A bunk bed and one twin were up against either wall. That left only enough room for one tall dresser that was piled high with clothing. Lindsey had been right. There wasn't any place to put all the stuff they were holding.

"Can we put it in Marnie's room?" Claudia suggested.

Lindsey shook her head. "That room is loaded with baby stuff."

"What about that closet?" Mallory asked, nodding toward the one closet in the corner.

"You could try," said Suzi.

Claudia went into the room, still holding her armful of stuffed animals, dolls, dress-up clothes, and books. She wriggled the fingers of her right hand free enough to pull at the doorknob.

Slowly, the closet door opened. With a rumble, and then a crash, an avalanche of toys fell on top of her. A huge, brown teddy bear bounced over the pile and knocked Claudia down, making her drop everything in her arms.

"Are you all right?" Mallory asked with laughter in her voice.

"I'm fine," said Claudia, rolling her eyes.

"I don't mean to laugh but you look funny sitting there buried under all that stuff," said Mallory as she cleared a stuffed jaguar and a plastic Minnie Mouse off Claudia.

"Where do you want us to put the rest of these things?" Suzi asked.

Claudia just shook her head as she climbed out of the pile. "I have absolutely no idea."

CHAPTER 6

On Friday morning, I shut off my alarm and fell back to sleep. Luckily, though, my eyes popped open while there was still enough time to make it to school. Enough time if I moved like lightning, that was.

I pulled on jeans, a blue workshirt, socks, and sneakers, and raced down the stairs. I came to a screeching halt when I reached the kitchen. Mary Anne stood at the counter eating a bowl of corn flakes dressed in a yellow sweat shirt dress, yellow stockings, and black flats. "Mary Anne, why are you dressed all in . . ." Then I remembered. "Class Color Day!" I cried.

Yellow was the eighth-grade color.

"I've been dying to wear this new dress somewhere so today seemed like a good opportunity," Mary Anne said with a hint of apology in her voice. I think she felt a little guilty about giving in to School Spirit Month after all the complaining she'd done.

I didn't blame her, though. If you have a great new yellow dress on a day when you're supposed to wear yellow, why not wear the dress?

I, however, didn't have anything yellow in my wardrobe. And I don't look particularly great in yellow. "Do you have anything else that's yellow?" I asked Mary Anne.

"I don't think so." Mary Anne put her bowl in the dishwasher. "Anyway, it's getting late."

"I'm going back upstairs to see if I can dig up *something* yellow," I said.

"You'd better be fast."

"Go ahead without me," I told Mary Anne.

"All right. Good luck."

I zoomed back upstairs and started pulling open my drawers. There was nothing yellow. Then I threw open the suitcase which still held my summery stuff from California. "Yellow! Yes!" I cried triumphantly as I snapped up a pair of yellow socks.

Hopping around the room, I yanked off my sneakers and socks, then flopped on the bed and put on the yellow socks. As soon as my sneakers were retied, I ran downstairs, grabbed my pack and heavy denim jacket from the living room closet, and practically flew out the front door.

The weird thing about being late is that nothing is where it's supposed to be. The man who is pulling out of his driveway when you go by every day is already gone. The lady who comes out to get her paper isn't there, but someone you've never seen before is walking a dog. They're small things, but somehow they put you off balance and remind you that you're late, late, late!

Besides noticing those things, my stomach was also growling. I almost never skip breakfast, and now I remembered why. I hated the empty feeling in the pit of my stomach.

I guess I'm telling you all this to help explain why I was in a crabby mood by the time I reached SMS.

I noticed that the buses that usually arrive last were still unloading kids. At least I'd made it. The next thing I noticed was a red and white van parked inside the gate. It was the WSBK van from Stoneybrook's local TV channel. A man with a large camera on his shoulder was taping students as they entered the school. A blonde woman in a red pants suit held a microphone and interviewed students as they came through the gate. I recognized her from TV. Her name was Mimi Snowden. She was talking to an eighth-grader named Grace Blume who was wearing a yellow rain slicker (even though there wasn't a cloud in the sky), yellow pants, and high-tops that she'd obviously painted yellow.

As I approached, I could see Grace smile and flip back her hair to reveal large, yellow daisy earrings.

I ducked my head, hoping I could slip quietly past Mimi Snowden and the cameraman.

"You! Young lady in the denim!" Mimi Snowden called to me.

I looked up and over — which was a mistake. I should have just kept going. But in that split second of hesitation, Mimi Snowden and the cameraman seemed to leap in front of me. "I notice that you're not wearing one particular color." The reporter got right to the point. "What grade are you in?"

"I'm in eighth," I said, feeling trapped. I lifted my pants to show my socks. "And I'm wearing yellow socks."

Mimi Snowden laughed pleasantly. "Oh, come on, now. Is that the best you can do? Where's your school spirit?"

"I forgot what day it was," I said brusquely. I guess I could have been friendlier, but I was late, I was hungry, and I didn't feel like having to explain myself to a stranger, even if it was Mimi Snowden.

"Well, at least you're honest," Mimi Snowden said with that warm smile she always wears. (A smile which always looks fake to me.)

Almost instantly, she forgot about me, turning her back as she faced the camera. She said something into the camera but I didn't bother to stick around to hear. Instead, I jogged the rest of the way across the parking lot to the back entrance.

As I reached the back door, Alan Gray was going in. "Hey, Dawn, I love all the yellow you're wearing," he said. "It shows a lot of school spirit."

Alan Gray is kind of a jerk, but he *was* in yellow, sort of. He'd pinned blown-up yellow balloons all over his jacket and was wearing yellow plaid pants that were way too big for him, probably his father's.

"It looks like you have enough spirit for everybody," I replied, trying not to sound cranky about it. (Although cranky is how I was feeling.)

"Yeah, sure," he said, unamused. Several kids who were going into school behind us gave me sour looks.

By the time I reached my homeroom, three other kids had made cracks about my lack of yellow.

"Oh, the yellow is blinding me," said Bruce Schermerhorn as I slid into my seat just as the bell rang.

Bruce, who was dressed in a yellow football jersey, is a good guy, and I know he was just teasing, but I was out of patience. "I forgot! Okay?" I snapped.

"Okay, okay," he said.

"Sorry," I mumbled. I stuck my foot out into the aisle and hiked up my jeans to show my socks.

"Oh, the subtle approach," he said, nodding. "I see."

At the front of the class I noticed that Shawna Riverson had forgotten to wear yellow, too. Two other kids, Mary Sherwood and Katie Shea, were trying to tape yellow construction paper on her. Shawna wanted nothing to do with it, and was swatting them off as if they were flies. "Get out of here with that!" she told them.

"Why don't you leave her alone," said Mary Anne, who sat close to Shawna.

Katie and Mary ignored Mary Anne. "What's the matter, Shawna? Too cool for Color Day?" Katie asked, clearly annoyed.

As she spoke, she noticed me. "Dawn!" she said, her eyes lighting with malicious enthusiasm. "You need some yellow, too."

Luckily for me, Mr. Blake walked in just then and told everyone to sit down. I was *not* going to spend the day with yellow construction paper taped to me.

While Mr. Blake took attendance, I saw Katie folding construction paper. She made two yellow paper hats and handed one to Shawna and slid one down the aisle to me. Mary Anne turned around and rolled her eyes at me. Easy for her! She was ablaze in yellow. But I appreciated the sympathy.

I wasn't about to pick up the ridiculous hat, but Bruce did. He put it on his head and crossed his eyes at me. "Very funny," I whispered. I saw Shawna push the hat to the side of her desk.

Homeroom was just the beginning. For the rest of the day everywhere I went, someone had something to say about my clothes. I wasn't alone, though. Quite a number of kids had forgotten to wear yellow (or red if they were sixth-graders, or green if they were in the seventh grade), and all of them were getting a hard time from kids who did wear their class color.

At lunchtime, Emily Bernstein, who is in eighth grade and was not wearing yellow, told me some kids from the pep squad sprayed her locker with yellow funny foam. Even Kristy and Claudia bugged me about not wearing yellow. (I noticed that over at her "mature friend" table, Stacey wasn't in yellow, either, but her boyfriend, Robert, was.) Kristy was particularly annoying. "What is the big deal about showing some school spirit?" she said with an edge to her voice.

"How does wearing yellow prove anything?" I countered. "Does it help the school or the team in any way?"

"It's a symbol," Kristy insisted.

"A symbol of what?"

"Spirit."

"Well, what exactly is spirit? Wearing yellow for this event doesn't show you care about your school. Doing things in support of the school shows you care," I said. "Besides why should one grade be pitted against another? Is it some kind of competition over which grade has the most spirit?"

"Yes!" Kristy said.

"Then that's dumb," I replied.

"You just don't get it," she said, shaking her head in dismay.

She was right. I didn't get it.

When I went back to my locker after lunch, it was also covered with yellow foam. The pep squad had struck again.

By the time I returned home, I was in the worst mood I could remember in a long time. I'd started out the day feeling bad about forgetting to wear yellow, but now I felt mad. I couldn't believe how awful our classmates had acted toward us kids who forgot about Color Day. It was horrible!

I was glad that our BSC meeting was busy. It left us *no* time to discuss Color Day. The phone just kept ringing. Mary Anne stuck to business and said very little that didn't have to do with baby-sitting. She and Shannon took a job for the DeWitt-Barrett crew. "Is there anything we can bring to make the situation better over there?" she wondered aloud.

"Bring a bigger house," said Claudia.

"Definitely don't bring Kid-Kits," Mallory said. "They won't fit inside."

Mary Anne sighed and nodded. Then she went back to looking through the record book, but her expression told me she was thinking about something else entirely.

At home, she ran straight to her room. Sensing she was upset about something, I went after her.

"Can I come in?" I asked, knocking on her door. Her reply was a hiccuppy kind of sob. I cracked the door open. "You okay?"

Mary Anne wiped her eyes and waved me in. "I'm upset about what happened today at school, about Color Day," she managed to say.

I sat on the bed beside her and patted her shoulder. "It's all right. I got through it. It was a pain, but it wasn't that bad. It's nice of you to be so concerned about my feelings and — "

"I'm not," Mary Anne blurted out, then began crying again.

Now I was confused. "What's the matter then?"

"Pajama Day! I mean, I'm sorry about what happened to you today, but it just showed me that I *have* to participate in Pajama Day. Look what a hard time you got for today, and you even had yellow socks on. If I wear regular clothing on Pajama Day the other kids will make fun and be mad. I can't face doing it and I can't face not doing it."

"Mary Anne, the more I think about Spirit Month, the more I think that — "

"Dawn! Mary Anne!" Mom called from downstairs. "Come down here, quick."

Mary Anne wiped her eyes on the blanket. She and I hurried downstairs. Richard and Mom were in front of the TV, watching the six-thirty news. "They're covering Spirit Month at your school," Mom said excitedly.

Mary Anne and I sat on the floor to watch. Mimi Snowden stood on the SMS grounds in her red pants suit. "Not only is Stoneybrook Middle School launching a full scale Spirit Month, but their arch rival, Howard Township Middle School, is having one as well. Both schools will be worked up to a fever pitch by the time of the big baseball game. We're here at Stoneybrook Middle School today to see how the students really feel about School Spirit Month."

First she talked to a boy named Robbie Mara, a sixth-grader dressed in a red sweat-suit. Then they spoke to Grace Blume in her yellow slicker. "Not all the students share their classmates' enthusiasm for School Spirit Month," Mimi Snowden said seriously. "Take this young lady, for example."

"Dawn! It's you!" cried Mom.

I cringed and hung my head. Why did I have to be the one representing kids who weren't in the spirit of things?

It was strange to see myself on TV. Boy, did I ever look annoyed and crabby! The only part of the interview they played was when I said, "I forgot what day it was," in that cranky voice. They didn't even show my yellow socks.

Then Mimi Snowden faced the camera. At that point I'd walked away and hadn't heard what she was saying. I heard it now.

"Students like the one we just talked to are not typical of the high-spirited Stoneybrook students. And that's a lucky thing for the school and the kids who are giving their all for School Spirit Month at Stoneybrook Middle School. Tomorrow, a look at how Spirit Month is going at Howard Township Middle School."

"The nerve!" Mom cried.

"You didn't tell me you were going to be

on the news," said Mary Anne.

"I forgot," I said honestly.

"That seems to be your big line for the day," Richard kidded with a smile.

"Don't laugh, Richard," Mom said. "That woman had no right to say what she said about Dawn. I'm calling the station and complaining. It's shameful for a professional to exploit a young person like that."

"The damage is already done," said Richard.

"I'm complaining anyway." Mom headed for the phone.

"This is terrible, terrible, terrible," Mary Anne muttered, getting up. "She shouldn't have said that about you. You have plenty of school spirit, real spirit, not all this jerky, ridiculous, embarrassing stuff. I wish we could just get rid of the whole thing."

"Start a petition, get rid of it," Mom called from the kitchen.

Mary Anne and I looked at one another, our eyes wide. "Do you think we could?" Mary Anne asked.

"We could try," I said.

CHAPTER 7

By Monday morning, Mary Anne and I had drafted a petition to do away with the rest of School Spirit Month. Here's what it said: *We, the undersigned, petition for the immediate elimination of School Spirit Month. We feel that the activities are dividing the student body in an unhealthy way and are sometimes even demeaning. Real school spirit is promoted by a sincere respect and concern for the well-being of all students. In calling for the end of School Spirit Month, we feel we are demonstrating our true school spirit and not some false show of meaningless zeal.*

"False show of meaningless zeal." Mary Anne stood in my bedroom doorway and re-read the petition, which was written on a yellow legal pad, for the millionth time as I got ready for school. "I like that phrase," she said. "It really says it."

I knew she was nervous. I'm better at standing up for my beliefs than Mary Anne is. It comes more naturally to me and I've had more experience doing it. Mary Anne always wants everyone to be happy. But she seemed determined to go through with the petition.

"Good luck with your petition today," said Mom when we came down to the kitchen. "I give you girls a lot of credit."

"After that news report everyone knows I have no school spirit anyway," I said, grabbing a handful of granola.

"Don't remind me," said Mom angrily. "I'm still waiting for Mimi Snowden to call me back. If she doesn't call me today, I'm going to call her and giving her a piece of my mind. Maybe I'll write a letter to the *Stoneybrook News*, too."

Maybe I get my fighting spirit from Mom.

We arrived at school early so we could pass our petition around before homeroom. "There's Emily Bernstein," I said, spotting Emily entering the office of the school paper, the *SMS Express*, of which she's the editor. "Emily!" I called to her. "Wait."

Mary Anne and I showed her our petition. "I will gladly sign this," said Emily, writing her name in bold letters.

"What's that?" asked a girl named Julie Stern who does layouts for the *Express*. We showed her the petition and she nodded enthusiastically as she signed. "I'm glad someone is doing something about this stupid idea.

I resent having my class time used up, especially study hall."

"Not to mention all the schoolwork we're missing over this dumbness," added Emily. "What's the big event today?"

"Make a New Friend Day," Julie replied. "We're having a big assembly in the gym and you're supposed to introduce yourself to someone you've never met."

"That's not so bad," I said.

"Yeah, but tomorrow is Dress Like a Teacher Day," said Emily. "I have a deadline to meet on the paper. I'll be here till six, then I have a test to study for. I don't have time to start rigging up some costume." Emily's eyes grew bright with an idea. "Let me type this on one of the computers, then I'll make copies and give them to other kids to pass around."

"Great idea," Mary Anne said.

I was glad Emily and Julie were behind us. Maybe more kids than we knew would be willing to sign our petition.

When Emily was done retyping our petition, Mary Anne and I headed for homeroom. I stopped Shawna Riverson outside class and she was happy to sign, too.

While Shawna was signing, Katie Shea stopped by. "What's that? A petition?"

"Yeah, a petition to stop Maniac Month." Shawna spit out the words.

Katie went pale. "You mean School Spirit Month?"

"We feel that it's causing more trouble than good," I said, trying to sound reasonable and smooth over Shawna's hostility.

"You're nuts!" Katie cried. "School Spirit Month is the best thing that's ever happened to this school." Katie's eyes narrowed at me. "I saw you on TV last night. You just want the news people to come back here and put you on TV again."

"That's not true," I said.

Mary Sherwood was going into class and Katie ran to her side. "Wait till I tell you about this," she said to Mary, sending Mary Anne, Shawna, and me a scathing glare.

"Uh-oh," said Mary Anne. "Pretty soon everyone's going to know about this."

"So what!" cried Shawna indignantly. "It's a free country. You can circulate a petition if you want."

"I know." I sighed. "I just hope kids like Katie don't get too nasty about it."

"Well, Katie was certainly nasty enough," said Shawna.

For the rest of the morning, in between classes, I tried to give the petition only to kids I thought would be sympathetic, but the news was out. I noticed kids staring at me in the hall.

At lunchtime I discovered the words *Go Back to California You Weirdo* scrawled on my locker in black marker. I stood staring at it in disbelief. Who would do something like that? It was creepy.

"What a jerk," said a familiar voice behind me.

I turned and saw Stacey looking at the writing. "Hi," I said, feeling uncomfortable. Stacey and I hadn't been speaking since she left the BSC.

"Hi," she replied stiffly. "Someone told me you have a petition I want to sign."

"You mean this?" I asked, handing her the paper.

"Yeah." She read it quickly and signed. "I love the word zeal," she said as she handed it back to me.

I nodded. "Thanks for signing."

"Sorry about your locker," she said. "See ya."

"See ya."

I watched her hurry down the hall and disappear into a stairwell. There was something about seeing my former friend walking away, and then looking back at the mean writing on my locker that got to me. Tears started to tingle in my eyes. I jammed the heels of my hands into my eyes to stop them. This wasn't a time for crying.

Opening my locker, I found a wrinkled bandanna I'd left in there and tried wiping off the writing. All I succeeded in doing was smearing it.

In the lunchroom, Kristy and Claudia gave Mary Anne and me a very chilly greeting when we sat down. "Where's Logan?" Mary Anne asked.

"He said he had a meeting. Something about the baseball team," said Kristy. "But maybe he just wasn't in the mood to see you right now."

"Kristy!" I cried.

"Well, who would blame him," said Kristy. "Here he is on a great winning baseball team and his girlfriend is going around trying to wreck School Spirit Month."

"Logan always tells me to do what I think is right," replied Mary Anne.

"How can you think what you're doing is right?" Kristy asked angrily. "Either of you?"

"I think you're both taking this too seriously," Claudia put in more mildly. "It's just for fun."

"We think it's right because it *is* right," I said firmly.

"Who are you kidding?" exclaimed Kristy. "Mary Anne is just too uptight to wear pajamas to school, that's all. And Dawn, you're not happy unless you have some cause to crusade for. This time, you picked the wrong cause. Give it up. It's going to cause big trouble. I'm telling you this as a friend."

"No, you're not! You're ordering me as president of the BSC. Well, this isn't the BSC right now!"

"And I am *not* uptight!" Mary Anne added, her face growing red.

I couldn't remember ever feeling that angry at Kristy. I was so mad my hands were trembling and my face was hot. I pushed my chair back. "I think I'll eat lunch somewhere else," I said.

"Wait for me," said Mary Anne.

We stormed over to a table halfway across the cafeteria and sat down. Mary Anne's eyes were red-rimmed. "Are you sure we *are* doing the right thing?" she asked.

"Yes," I said hotly. "If what we're doing is so threatening and making kids — even our friends — behave this badly, then it has to be right."

The afternoon was a mix of positive and negative reactions. By the second to last period Mary Anne and I had collected fifty signatures. Emily Bernstein was sure to have even more. We were doing pretty well.

When I arrived at the gym for Make a New Friend Day, it was crammed with kids, all milling around.

The voice of Mr. Taylor, the principal, came over the PA system. He gave a speech about the success of School Spirit Month so far. Then he instructed everyone to go make a new friend. "Spend the rest of the school day getting to know your new friend. You are free to walk outside on the school grounds if you wish."

I looked around for someone I didn't know. I know a lot of kids, so it took a little doing. I spotted a short blonde girl standing alone. She looked like she might be a seventh-grader. I headed toward her.

"Hi," I said, extending my hand. "I'm Dawn Schafer and I'd like to — "

"Dawn Schafer," the girl cried in a disgusted voice. "No, thanks. I don't want to be *your* new friend." She turned her back on me and walked off.

I was standing there recovering from the shock when someone tapped my shoulder. I turned and saw a plump girl with long black hair looking up at me. When I smiled at her, she jumped back in alarm. "Oh, no, never mind," she said. "I didn't know it was you. I saw you on TV last night. Never mind." With that, she hurried off into the crowd of kids.

Feeling very unpopular, I gazed around, looking for Mary Anne. I saw some boy walking away from her. It looked like she was having the same trouble I was.

I hurried over to her. "Want to get out of here?" I asked her.

"Yes," Mary Anne said decisively.

We left the crowd of kids and walked down the hall to the back door of the school. It felt good to leave the hot, airless gym and be outside in the warm April air.

We'd just stepped out the door when something yellow whizzed past my head. If I hadn't ducked, it would have hit me. Instead, the yellow water balloon splattered on the school wall behind Mary Anne and me.

"Heads up, girls," Alan Gray called. "Too bad I didn't get your petition."

CHAPTER 8

After that, things did not go smoothly at all. Our BSC meeting that afternoon was very tense. We spoke to one another only about baby-sitting business.

The next day, Mary Anne and I intentionally didn't come to school dressed as teachers. And when I saw the kinds of outfits the kids were wearing, I was glad we'd boycotted the event.

One boy wore an ugly mask and a huge pocket pencil holder, obviously mocking a science teacher named Mr. Harold, who isn't too good-looking. I happen to think Mr. Harold is pretty nice even if he isn't handsome.

I saw another boy dressed as a woman teacher who happens to be heavy. He had padded himself to look super fat.

There were endless insulting outfits. What was the point? To embarrass the teachers? That sure showed school spirit.

By Tuesday everyone knew about the petition. Lots of kids were dying to sign it. I was constantly being stopped in the hall by kids I didn't even know. Emily Bernstein told me they were crowding into the *SMS Express* office to sign before homeroom. Mary Anne got our own copy of the petition so we could rustle up more signatures.

And the kids who were for School Spirit Month were really mad at us. When Mary Anne and I handed the petition to a boy named Trevor Sandbourne, another boy Bruce Jamison, ripped it out of his hands. He was about to tear it up when Logan came along and yanked it back from him. "I don't think that belongs to you, Bruce," he said.

Bruce glared at Logan. "What's the matter, Bruno? Is your girlfriend telling you what to do now?"

Logan handed the petition back to Mary Anne. "She's entitled to her opinion," Logan said calmly.

"You should be embarrassed to go out with her," Bruce snarled as he loped off down the hall.

"What a lowlife," Trevor sneered.

"Thanks," Mary Anne said to Logan.

"No problem. This *is* still America. You do have a right to say what you like."

Unfortunately, a lot of kids didn't think we had that right. I found a hate letter stuffed in my locker at the end of the day. I won't bother to repeat all the things it said. The most frightening part was the last sentence. *Some people could get hurt if this petition isn't stopped.*

My brain whirled in disbelief. Someone was actually threatening to hurt Mary Anne and me over this. These couldn't be the same kids I went to school with every day. They just couldn't be.

But they were.

When we arrived at school the next day I saw that the *SMS Express* office was crowded. Emily saw Mary Anne and me, and waved us over. "Kids today are telling me that they wouldn't be signing except that they're so disgusted by the way the pro-Spirit Month kids are acting that they don't want to have anything to do with them or with Spirit Month."

I looked in at the *Express* office and was pleased at the number of kids I saw. I didn't feel so alone. No matter how nasty the Spirit Month kids got, they didn't represent the entire school. That made me feel better about my classmates.

At lunchtime, Kristy wasn't at our table. Claudia was, though. "Kristy said she's got to study," Claudia explained.

I frowned skeptically. Kristy never skips lunch to study. "She just doesn't want to sit with us, does she?" I said.

Claudia shrugged. "You *are* making a lot of people mad and she doesn't agree with what you're doing. But maybe she really had to study."

"She didn't," I said. "What about you? What do you think?"

"I think you and Mary Anne are making a lot of trouble for no good reason," Claudia said honestly. "The entire school is dividing up over this."

I saw Logan and Mary Anne walk by. Mary Anne stopped at the table. "Logan and I are going to eat lunch alone today," she said. "We need to talk."

"Okay," I replied.

I was about to turn my attention back to Claudia when I noticed a bunch of kids wearing large, round paper buttons saying: *Support Spirit Month!* They made sure to glare at me as they went by.

I was still looking at them when suddenly I was covered with something wet and gooey. I jumped up and saw that it was spaghetti in meat sauce, which was on the hot lunch menu that day. Whirling around, I found myself face-to-face with Alan Gray. "Oops, I forgot," he smirked. "You're a vegetarian, aren't you, Dawn?"

I was so furious and embarrassed that I was speechless.

But Claudia grabbed the chocolate pudding from her tray and hurled it at Alan. He ducked to the side and the pudding headed for the fuzzy pink sweater of a girl sitting behind Alan, landing smack, dab on her *Support Spirit Month* button.

Infuriated, the girl jumped up and threw her entire plate of spaghetti across the table. She was aiming at Claudia, but the spaghetti flew all over the place. A meatball bounced off Alan's head. "Hey! I'm on your side!" he shouted at her.

It was all over from there on. Food flew around the cafeteria. It wasn't a funny food fight, either. It was an angry food fight. I ducked under the table and made sure to put my petition into my backpack. I didn't want to risk anything happening to it.

When I climbed out from underneath, I ducked in time to avoid being hit with a clump of green Jell-O. I saw a boy push another boy into a cluster of chairs.

Then several shrill whistles blew from different corners of the cafeteria. Mr. De Young, the boys' gym teacher, hurried to the center of the cafeteria crying: "Break it up! Break it up!"

Mr. Kingbridge and Mrs. Rosenauer, another gym teacher, also moved in to calm things down.

In minutes, Mr. Halprin, the janitor, was there with a bucket and mop, but Mr. Kingbridge stopped him. "All we need are rags and buckets. The kids will clean this up."

We spent the rest of the lunch period cleaning up the mess, each side blaming the other for what had happened.

During the next period, Mr. Taylor's voice came on the PA system. "The regularly scheduled Spirit Month activity, that is the preparation for Mural Day, has been postponed. Instead, an open forum will be held in the auditorium during the last two school periods to discuss the controversy over Spirit Month. Attendance is not mandatory. Those not wishing to attend, please report to the gym for an open study hall."

I was glad to hear this. Now we'd be able to get everything out in the open.

Even though no one *had* to go to the forum, it sure looked as if everyone were there. Emily found Mary Anne and me before we went into the auditorium. "This is the time to present the petition," she said. "Mr. Taylor will be there. So will Mr. Kingbridge. We'll do it out in the open and no one can accuse us of being sneaky."

Mary Anne, Emily, and I had collected three hundred signatures in the last few days. "Who wants to present it?" I asked.

"Not me," Mary Anne said quickly.

"I do, but I think you should, Dawn," said Emily. "You and Mary Anne started this."

"All right," I agreed, taking the petition pages from her. "I will."

The three of us entered the auditorium together. On the stage, sitting at tables, were Mr. Taylor; Mr. Kingbridge; Mrs. Gonzalez, my science teacher; Mrs. Rosenauer; Ms. Harris, my gym teacher; and Mrs. Pinelli, who is a music teacher.

The pro-Spirit Month kids grouped themselves on the right side of the auditorium, and the kids against it sat on the left. I looked around and saw Jessi, Claudia, and Kristy on the right. Mallory was on the left toward the front. I noticed Stacey on the left, not too far from Mallory, but her boyfriend, Robert, was on the right.

"This is like the Civil War, with friends divided against one another," Emily noted as we moved to seats toward the front of the auditorium.

Mr. Taylor addressed the students from a microphone set up at the center of the stage. "Welcome, students," he said. "Before this controversy goes further, we want to hear all the facts, all your opinions. Then we've assembled a faculty panel to make a decision regarding the final fate of School Spirit Month.

We will base our decision on what we hear today. To speak, please come to the podium set up in the center aisle, and say your piece. Keep your message brief. Thank you."

Kids began pouring into the aisles, lining up to speak at the podium. "Get up there," Emily urged me. "You should be one of the first."

Clutching the petition, I did my best to scramble toward the front of the line. "Don't push," Grace Blume snapped at me. "Wait your turn."

"I wasn't pushing," I snapped back.

The first one to speak was Katie Shea. "The decent kids at SMS love Spirit Month," she shouted into the microphone. The entire right side of the auditorium broke out in cheers and whistles. "We don't want a bunch of no-spirit weirdos blocking us in showing our love for our school."

"You're the weirdo!" shouted Shawna Riverson from the left side.

Then the left side of the auditorium cheered.

"We want Spirit Month to stay!" Katie shouted.

The right side started chanting. "Spir-it Month! Spir-it Month!"

Mr. Taylor went to his microphone and quieted them. "Let's hear from the next speaker, please," he instructed.

Logan spoke next. "As a member of the SMS

baseball team, I want to remind everyone that the real reason for Spirit Month is to support our team that so far this season has been undefeated and — "

"Sit down, you wimp!" yelled Bruce Jamison.

"And really needs your support at the big Howard Township game this month," Logan continued.

"What's your point, Mr. Bruno?" asked Mr. Taylor from the stage.

"I guess my point is just that we should remember why we're doing this."

"Your point is well taken," said Mr. Taylor. "Next speaker, please."

The next three speakers were all pro-Spirit Month. The two after them were against it. None of them said much except that they did or didn't want Spirit Month to continue.

Finally, it was my turn. "Sit down, you California freak," some boy from the right shouted.

I looked over sharply. He was probably the person who marked up my locker. I couldn't see who had shouted, though.

Clearing my throat, I leaned toward the microphone. "I have a petition here containing three hundred signatures," I began.

Wild booing started up from the right side.

"Quiet, please!" Mr. Taylor spoke sternly.

The booing stopped.

I read the petition, then I handed it to Mr. Taylor on the stage. "Three hundred signatures prove that it's not just a few of us who are unhappy about School Spirit Month," I continued, back at the podium. "And, I'd like to add that I've been threatened, assaulted with a water balloon, and insulted just for trying to express my opinion about this. I don't think that says much about school spirit or the spirit of decency or any other kind of spirit."

The kids on the left cheered and clapped as I left the podium.

I was returning to my seat when a rubber band snapped the corner of my cheek. Someone on the right had shot it at me. I turned, holding my cheek. "Who did that?" I asked angrily.

No one replied. A few kids smirked at me.

I never realized standing up for what you believe in could be so hard and hurtful.

CHAPTER 9

The Barrett-DeWitt kids keep you
going every second. And today they
were all over the place trying to prove
that their house isn't too small. They're
determined not to move, no matter what.

*I was really not in
the mood for what
happened. I've had
enough of protests for
a lifetime.*

On Saturday, Shannon and Mary Anne baby-sat for the Barrett-DeWitt kids. When they arrived, the house was in the same disheveled condition as when Claudia and Mallory had been there.

Once again, Mrs. DeWitt didn't look too good, either. She dashed upstairs and in about fifteen minutes had pulled herself together somewhat. Still, she wasn't her usual glamorous self. "I'm just meeting Franklin for lunch at the Rosebud Cafe. We won't be long," she said. As Mrs. DeWitt left, Shannon had the same feeling Claudia had had — that Mrs. DeWitt was actually fleeing the chaotic house.

Shannon wondered about this, since Mrs. DeWitt never minded messes much before. Maybe it was something different this time. Was she overwhelmed by the number of kids in the house? Or was it the house itself?

Shannon told me that within minutes of Mrs. DeWitt's departure, she detected a secretive undercurrent among the kids. There was a lot of whispering and scurrying from room to room. "What do you think is up?" she asked Mary Anne.

Mary Anne shrugged wearily. (She hadn't been herself since the forum on Wednesday.) "Come here, you guys," Mary Anne called to Marnie and Ryan who were toddling around the floor. She sat them in front of her and began playing a clapping game with them.

Shannon realized it would be up to her to find out what was going on with the other kids. It didn't take long. She found them in the basement in Buddy's and Taylor's room. As she was going down the stairs she heard Buddy telling the others: "And then Mom said, 'This just isn't working, Franklin. I'm losing my mind!'"

"I know," said Suzi. "You can't find anything in this house."

"That's not what she meant," Buddy told her. "She means living in this house is driving her crazy!"

Suzi gasped. "Mommy is going crazy?"

Unnoticed, Shannon stopped at the bottom of the stairs to listen to the rest of the conversation.

"She's not going crazy," Lindsey said sensibly. "She was just mad because Buddy stayed in the shower for five years while she was getting ready to meet Daddy for lunch."

"It wasn't five years," Buddy insisted.

"Okay, then, four years. And she said there was no hot water by the time she did get in."

"Is Daddy going crazy, too?" Taylor asked Lindsey.

"Definitely," Lindsey began. Then she noticed Shannon, and stopped talking. "Hi!" she greeted Shannon.

"Can I be part of this meeting?" Shannon asked.

"I guess," Lindsey said. She turned back to her brother. "Daddy said he understood exactly how she felt, which means he must be losing his mind, too. He said he was tired of never being able to find anything. *And* he said he plans to do something about it."

"What? What?" asked Suzi eagerly.

"I don't know. They started talking real low. Buddy and I couldn't hear them anymore."

"We think they're going to make us move," Buddy said ominously, his eyes wide.

"No!" yelled Taylor. "We're not moving!"

"No way, José!" cried Suzi.

"Uh-uh," said Madeleine, shaking her head.

"Wait a minute," said Shannon. "You don't know that they want to move. They didn't say that."

"What else could Daddy mean?" asked Lindsey. "What else is there to *do* about it?"

Shannon didn't know the answer to that one. What Lindsey said made sense. "Maybe it won't be so bad. You might just move down the block, or around the corner."

"No, we'll move out of town," said Buddy assuredly. "Mom says Stoneybrook is too expensive. She says they could afford a bigger house somewhere else, but not in Stoney-brook.''

"Maybe if you kids didn't leave your toys all over the place it wouldn't be so bad," said Shannon.

"If we cleaned up, do you think they'd let us stay?" asked Lindsey.

"I don't know. It might help."

"We tried to clean up when Claudia and Mallory were here, but it didn't work." Lindsey sighed. "We have way too much stuff."

"Is there anything you could get rid of?" Shannon suggested.

"I guess," said Buddy.

"You could donate some toys to the Salvation Army," Shannon said.

"For children who don't have any toys?" asked Suzi.

"Yes," Shannon replied.

"We could try," Lindsey said gamely.

The girls hurried up the stairs while Buddy and Taylor started pulling games off the stack. "We could get rid of some of these," said Buddy. "We never play some of them."

Shannon ran upstairs and found a black plastic garbage bag for Buddy and Taylor. "I want to keep the Cootie game," Taylor was saying as she handed Buddy the bag.

"When's the last time you played it?" Shannon asked.

"Three days ago," Taylor answered.

"Then keep it, but give away anything you haven't played in about a month," she suggested.

"Okay," Taylor agreed.

Shannon went back to the kitchen, got another bag, and went upstairs to help Madeleine, Suzi, and Lindsey sort through their things.

As they worked, Shannon was amazed at how many toys they were willing to part with. Apparently the idea of moving was enough to make them serious about cleaning. In less than half an hour the black bag was filled and Shannon went down for another.

In the kitchen, she met Buddy and Taylor lugging their full bag onto the linoleum floor. "We can put this stuff in the garage for now," said Buddy. "At least that will get it out of the house."

Inspired by that idea, Shannon grabbed more plastic bags and ran back upstairs. The girls had already filled one bag with books, toys, and games. "I'll take that out to the garage for you," Shannon offered.

"What's going on?" Mary Anne asked as Shannon returned from the garage.

Shannon explained the situation to her.

"I could take the babies upstairs and put them in the playpen in Marnie's room," Mary Anne said. "Then I'll try to make some order in there."

"Great," said Shannon.

In an hour, all the bedrooms looked *much* better. Mary Anne was even making headway in Marnie's room: folding up two electric swing chairs that weren't in use; throwing toys into a bassinet Marnie no longer uses; and generally making neater piles of things.

"Now you have to tackle the living room," Shannon told the kids.

The kids ran around gathering the toys off the living room floor. They scurried back to their rooms and were able to find places for all of them, since now their rooms were no longer overstuffed.

"Good work," Shannon congratulated them in the living room when they were done.

"But is it good enough?" Lindsey wondered. "Will it make them change their minds about moving? There's still only one bathroom, and no bedroom for Ryan."

"I know!" Buddy cried. "When Nicky Pike and his brothers and sisters didn't like the play Mallory wrote about them, they picketed."

"What did they pick?" asked Madeleine.

"They didn't pick anything," said Buddy. "They picketed. You know. They marched around in front of Mallory's room with signs saying her play was unfair to them."

"We could make signs saying it's unfair to make us move!" cried Lindsey.

"Are you sure that's a good idea?" Shannon asked.

"Definitely! It will show we mean business."

The next thing Shannon knew, Buddy and Lindsey were bringing posterboard into the living room. Suzi and Taylor brought in crayons and scissors. Soon, the kids were hard at work making signs. Even Madeleine did a rough drawing of herself standing outside her house with a heart over her head.

Mary Anne came downstairs with Marnie and Ryan. Her jaw dropped when she saw the kids taping their signs to sticks. "Mr. and Mrs. DeWitt might not be too thrilled to come home to this," she said.

"What can we do about it?" Shannon asked. "If we stop them now, we'll have a riot on our hands."

Mary Anne looked at her skeptically.

"All right, a *slight* exaggeration, but they've already finished their signs. At least their parents will know exactly how they feel and see that they're serious about it."

"That's true," Mary Anne agreed.

The kids picked up their signs and headed out to the front yard. Shannon followed them, checking her watch. It was fifteen minutes to two. Mrs. DeWitt had been gone over two hours. She and Mr. DeWitt would probably be home soon. Shannon wondered how they'd respond to this unexpected protest.

The kids sat cross-legged on the lawn for about fifteen minutes until their parents pulled into the driveway. Then they jumped to their feet and began walking back and forth in front of the door. "No! No! We won't go!" Buddy started chanting. The others took up the cry.

Mr. and Mrs. DeWitt looked at their children with puzzled expressions. "They don't want to move," Shannon explained.

"Why do they think we're moving?" Mrs. DeWitt asked.

Suzi put down her sign. "Because you're losing your mind in this house!" she cried dramatically.

Mrs. DeWitt burst out laughing.

Mr. DeWitt smiled broadly.

"What's so funny?" asked Lindsey indignantly.

"We're not moving," said Mr. DeWitt.

"But it's true, I am losing my mind," Mrs. DeWitt said through her laughter.

"But Buddy and I heard you talking, Daddy," Lindsey said. "You said you would *do* something about it."

"We're planning something all right," said Mr. DeWitt. "But it isn't a move."

CHAPTER 10

On Monday morning, as I walked by the *SMS Express* office on the way to my locker, Emily came out and stopped me. "You won't believe what I heard from a friend of mine last night," she said. "The kids over at Howard Township Middle School are going through the same thing we are here. They're totally divided over Spirit Month and they even had a big meeting in their gym to discuss it."

"Wow," I said. That *was* pretty interesting news. "It just proves the idea of School Spirit Month is a bad one. It causes trouble anywhere they try it."

"No kidding," said Emily.

I checked the hall clock. "I'd better get to my locker before homeroom. See ya."

When I reached my locker, I worked my combination, but the door wouldn't open. I tried the combination again, this time slowly, and still it wouldn't open. Frustrated, I yanked on my locker door, rattling the handle.

I spotted Mr. Halprin at the other end of the hall and ran to him. "Mr. Halprin, can you help me?" I asked. "My locker won't open."

"Let's take a look," he said, following me back to my locker. I told him my combination, and he tried the lock. "This lock is open," he said to me. "I heard all three clicks."

"Then why won't the door open?" I asked.

Mr. Halprin pulled at the door. Then he took a screwdriver from his tool belt and tried to pry the door open. Next he stuck his face close to the opening of the door and sniffed. "Glue," he said.

"What?"

"Someone has glued your door shut with a heavy bonding glue."

"Oh, no!" I cried. "What am I going to do?"

"I'll have to try to break the seal with a razor and some solvent," Mr. Halprin said, looking disgusted.

The bell for homeroom rang. "How long will it take?" I asked anxiously.

Mr. Halprin shook his head. "Can't say."

I had no choice but to go to homeroom without the books I needed, and still holding my pack. When I arrived there, I saw Mary Anne going in with her pack in her hands. "Someone glued your locker, too!" I cried angrily.

"Is that the problem?" Mary Anne said. "All

I know is that it wouldn't open."

"Glue," I confirmed. "Mr. Halprin is working on mine right now. You should go to my locker after class and ask him to open yours next."

"Who would do something so spiteful?"

"Half the student body at SMS," I reminded her. "The spirited half."

We went into homeroom and discovered Katie Shea walking around with a sign taped to her back. It said *Kick me if you believe in Spirit Month*.

I noticed the twinkle in Shawna Riverson's eyes and wondered if she'd taped the sign there. Obviously, Katie knew nothing about it.

At first it made me smile, but then I realized what it meant. The pro-spirit kids weren't the only ones playing dirty tricks. The anti-spirit kids were just as bad. Mary Sherwood finally noticed the sign, pulled it off Katie's back, and showed it to her. Both girls turned and glared at *me*.

Mr. Blake came in and asked everyone to sit down. After he took attendance, Mr. Taylor came onto the PA system. "I regret to tell you that the adults on our panel have failed to come to a conclusion regarding Spirit Month. I have been made aware that hostilities among students continue to run high. The panel has requested another meeting. Therefore, tomorrow night, at seven o'clock, a second meeting has been scheduled at the Stoneybrook High auditorium. Students are encouraged to attend with their parents. The faculty is also encouraged to be there. Let me add that until this issue is resolved, any students caught harassing other students will be firmly dealt with."

"Just what we need, *another* meeting," Mary muttered.

The rest of that morning was difficult without the books I needed. It took Mr. Halprin until after lunch to open my locker. Then he went to work on Mary Anne's.

Just before the second to last period, which was supposed to begin Mural Painting Day, Emily handed me a photocopied leaflet. *Protest Spirit Month*, it said. *Spend the last two periods in the cafeteria with students who feel the way you do.*

"Everyone from our side is coming," Emily told me excitedly.

"Does Mr. Taylor know about this?" I asked.

"He will," said Emily as she headed down the hall, handing out more leaflets.

I went to Mary Anne's locker to see how she was doing. She stood, looking anxious, while Mr. Halprin used a hammer to bang at the screwdriver he'd wedged into the locker opening.

"Are you going to this protest?" Mary Anne asked, jiggling her leaflet nervously.

"I suppose we should," I replied.

"Do you think we'll get in trouble?"

"I don't know." Mary Anne and I had started this. It was too late to back out. Besides, I didn't want to back out. I was committed to seeing this through.

"There," said Mr. Halprin as the door swung open.

"Sorry, Mr. Halprin," said Mary Anne. "This stupid prank was even more of a pain for you than for Dawn and me."

"You don't know the half of it," Mr. Halprin grumbled. "Yesterday someone dumped cooking oil in some poor girl's locker. I had to mop that up. All her things were ruined. Then another kid had feathers from a pillow dumped all over him. My staff spent an hour trying to vacuum up all the feathers. What a mess that was. When are you kids going to stop with this stupidity?"

That was a question we couldn't answer.

I shook my head. "Sorry about all the extra work this is causing."

Mr. Halprin just nodded. I couldn't blame him for being annoyed.

Mary Anne and I went down to the cafeteria and found it full of kids chanting: "Spirit Month must go!"

Mr. Kingbridge stuck his head in, rolled his eyes in dismay, and left. It looked as if we weren't going to get in trouble, anyway.

For the next two hours kids stood on chairs and spoke about why they thought Spirit Month was wrong. I got up and spoke. "If we let ourselves be forced to do things we don't believe in now," I said, "then all our lives we'll be people who allow ourselves to be pushed around. Is that the kind of people we want to be?"

"No! No! No!" the kids yelled.

"Then hang tough and we can win this thing!" I cried.

The kids clapped, cheered, and whistled for me. I felt as if I were leading the French Revolution or something thrilling like that.

By the end of those two periods I was filled with new resolve, determined to see this cause through no matter how ugly the other side wanted to be about it.

But as I leaned against a table and listened to the next speaker, a strange thought hit me. Our side was actually holding a sort of pep rally. It was an anti-pep pep rally, but the effect was pretty much the same. It made us feel good about our cause and determined to work that much harder for it.

I remembered Kristy saying to me, "You just don't get it."

Well, now I was beginning to get it — a small part of it, anyway. I still didn't see how anyone benefited from wearing pajamas to school. But I suddenly understood how enthusiasm, determination, and *spirit* could be pumped up by certain activities.

I pushed the thoughts away. It wasn't something I wanted to think about. I needed to stay firm in my anti-spirit position if I was going to keep working to abolish Spirit Month.

The protest ended with the final bell. On the way to my locker, I saw some of the new murals, still wet with glistening paint. Most of them were really good. I spotted one which was fantastic. It showed a tropical island, with dolphins jumping, seabirds, and people dancing in colorful costumes. It was the kind of place you'd want to escape to if you were having a really bad day. And it had the unmistakable mark of Claudia on it. I can recognize her artwork, and it was everywhere in this mural. She'd done a great job.

Our BSC meeting that afternoon might as well have taken place in a freezer; that's how chilly things were. Claudia, in particular, was tight-lipped and angry. Considering how beautifully her mural turned out, I was surprised that she was in such a bad mood.

"Why don't you tell Mary Anne, Dawn, and Mallory what happened today?" Kristy prompted her in a tense voice.

"My group did the most gorgeous mural," Claudia said, her eyes ablaze with anger. "After school I went back to take a last look at it. Some idiot had smeared the wet paint with a rag."

"The whole thing?" Mallory asked, aghast.

"No, but it was ruined," Claudia replied. "There were three big swipe marks across it."

I was so surprised. It must have happened right after I passed by the mural — when all the protest kids were leaving the cafeteria.

"How awful," murmured Jessi.

"That's a shame," said Mary Anne sadly.

"Oh, like you really care," Claudia snapped, turning her back on Mary Anne.

Instantly, tears welled in Mary Anne's eyes.

Logan, who was at that meeting, sat on the floor, hugging his knees. "You know what bothers me," he said quietly. "None of those murals had anything to do with baseball. I thought that the whole idea was to get everyone pumped up for the big game since we have a shot at the championship this year. We *are* still undefeated, you know."

"Baseball isn't exactly something beautiful to paint," Claudia said irritably.

Logan grew red and frowned, but he kept quiet.

"Gosh, this Spirit Month is sure causing a lot of trouble," said Shannon. "I hope they never have one at my school."

"No," Kristy said sharply. "You hope that if they have a School Spirit Month there aren't a lot of kids who don't understand school spirit and start making trouble."

"That is so unfair," I shot back.

"Hey, listen," Shannon said, her voice loud and anxious. "I found out what the DeWitts plan to do. I ran into Mrs. DeWitt today."

"What?" asked Mallory.

"They're not moving, they're building an addition to their house."

"What a good idea!" cried Mary Anne. "That will solve the problem and everyone will be happy."

It was as if Mrs. DeWitt knew we were talking about her family because just then the phone rang and she was on the other end. She needed two sitters for the following Saturday. She and Mr. DeWitt were throwing a groundbreaking party to celebrate the start of work on their new addition.

"Kristy, you're free," said Mary Anne after

consulting the record book. "So am I, so is Jessi, and so is Mallory."

Kristy folded her arms stubbornly. "No offense, but I'd rather not work with you right now, Mary Anne. I don't think it would go well."

Mary Anne pulled back as if Kristy had slapped her. She stared in disbelief at Kristy.

"And I'd rather not work with Kristy or Jessi," Mallory spoke up. "I don't think that would work either."

Mary Anne had to take a deep breath before she could speak again. "Then that leaves Kristy and Jessi to take the job together."

"Fine with me," said Kristy.

"Fine with me, too," Jessi agreed sullenly.

I envied the DeWitts for having found a solution that would keep everyone happy. Right now, it looked as though the students at SMS weren't going to be as lucky.

CHAPTER 11

I thought the School Spirit Month meeting in the auditorium was bad, but it was nothing compared to the big meeting held in the high school auditorium on Tuesday night.

Adults poured in with their kids. Not only were parents there, but Mimi Snowden from WSBK was back with *two* camera operators. A reporter and photographer from the *Stoneybrook News* were there. (I recognized them from the pep rally.) There was also a male reporter with a camera crew from a Stamford station. Several newspapers from outside Stoneybrook, including the *Howard Township Sun* were there, too.

I couldn't believe it. School Spirit Month had become big news.

Richard had to work late that night, but Mom attended the meeting with Mary Anne and me. As soon as we walked into the auditorium, Mimi Snowden spotted me. "There she is," she told her cameraman.

They rushed to me and Ms. Snowden stuck a microphone in my face. "Dawn Schafer, hello," she said. "We hear you and your step-sister are the ringleaders in the protest movement to — "

"Oh, no you don't," Mom said, stepping between Ms. Snowden and me. "After the way you misrepresented Dawn in the last broadcast, you're not speaking with her again. You haven't even had the courtesy to return my phone calls."

Ms. Snowden put on one of her trademark phony smiles. "And you must be Dawn's mother."

"I most certainly am."

Ms. Snowden angled herself between Mom and the cameraman. "Why not let your daughter air her views openly and not be restricted by . . ."

That was just the time Mary Anne and I needed to hurry down the aisle. Mom was right. I didn't need Mimi Snowden blowing things out of proportion and casting me as some kind of revolutionary.

As we neared the front, I noticed Jessi and her dad, Mr. and Mrs. Kishi with Claudia, and Kristy with her older brother Charlie and her stepfather Watson. They were all seated close together on the right. It was just like the other day, with the pro-Spirit Month people on the right, and the anti-Spirit Month people on the left.

We slipped into seats on the left, saving one for Mom. I looked around me and saw Stacey sitting with her mother and Robert. I suppose since Robert was with her now, he'd changed his position. Mallory was there, too, with Mrs. Pike.

Teachers were even sitting on opposite sides of the auditorium! On the right, I noticed Ms. Walden, a gym teacher; Mr. DeYoung, another gym teacher; my homeroom teacher, Mr. Blake; and Ms. Harris, my physical science teacher.

On the left I spotted: Mr. Dougherty, Mal's creative writing teacher; Mr. Fiske, who teaches English; Mr. Lehrer, Mrs. Simon, and Mrs. Hall, who also teach English.

The panel of teachers sat at a long table on the stage. Mr. Kingbridge and Mr. Taylor were in the middle. To their right were Mrs. Rosenaur and Ms. Harris. To the left were Mrs. Gonzalez, and Mrs. Pinelli. I could see now why they'd been unable to come to a conclusion. Obviously, the two gym teachers on the right were for School Spirit Month, while Mrs. Gonzalez and Mrs. Pinelli were against it. I'd even guess that Mr. Kingbridge and Mr. Taylor were divided on the issue.

"Settle down, people," Mr. Taylor said into his microphone. "Please settle down so we can begin."

People didn't settle down, though. They had already begun arguing among themselves.

"How dare you call my kid a juvenile delinquent!" a man behind me shouted at a man across the aisle on the right.

"Hey, if you can't get your kid to obey school rules, don't blame me," the man on the right shouted back.

"Yeah, well at least Jeffrey isn't a mindless robot. He can think for himself."

"People!" Mr. Taylor shouted. "Please settle down."

There was a low hum for a few more minutes, and then everyone did quiet down. "We don't have a podium today," Mr. Taylor said, "so I ask that you raise your hands and stand when I point to you. Please keep your comments brief as a lot of people here tonight wish to be heard."

Katie Shea's father stood up first and said that if kids couldn't even obey the rules of Spirit Month then how did the school expect to maintain any kind of order? "Some things you have to do because you're told to do them. Period. End of story," he said.

Lots of parents, mostly on the right, applauded this.

Alan Gray's mother got up and said that if we kids couldn't be forced to go along with Spirit Month, then we'd all start smoking, drinking, and taking drugs since we had no sense of values and by winning this protest we'd be given the go-ahead to do whatever we pleased. That struck me as pretty far-fetched, even ridiculous, but a lot of people clapped.

Mrs. Simon stood and complained that Spirit Month seriously cut into the time she had for teaching. "It's a real disaster for my curriculum," she said. "A wasted month really. For some students it will be a terrible setback."

Mr. Dougherty was the next to speak. "This is still America," he said passionately. "We teach our children that their destinies are in their hands, and then we turn around and lay down arbitrary laws and demand that they follow them."

"The key word is children, buddy," shouted a man from the right. "Children don't get to make rules in America or anywhere else."

"But this is a learning institution," Mr. Dougherty shot back. "What are we teaching our kids by forcing them to get in line?"

"We're teaching them to be good citizens," the other man replied angrily.

"Please, please," Mr. Taylor interrupted,

"we can't let this turn into a shouting match."

Mom slipped into the seat beside me. "I gave Mimi Snowden a piece of my mind," she said, looking satisfied.

Mr. Bruno was speaking. He said his son had worked hard as had his teammates, and that everyone seemed to be forgetting that School Spirit Month was originated to support the SMS baseball team. "The team is being divided and demoralized by all this hubbub," he said. "It's breaking down team morale completely. Eventually that's going to affect their game."

"Blame Dawn Schafer and Mary Anne Spier for that," shouted Mary Sherwood's mother.

Instantly, Mom was on her feet. "Now hold on!" she said to Mrs. Sherwood. "All these other people agree with my daughters. Don't you single them out!"

"Do you think what your girls did was right?"

"Yes, I do!" said Mom. "I'm proud of them." (There was a ripple of applause.)

"If you're proud, then you're not fit to be a mother," Mrs. Sherwood cried.

Mrs. Pike jumped to her feet. "Cindy, I think that's too harsh," she told Mrs. Sherwood. "I'm also proud of my daughter and of Mary Anne and Dawn, and I certainly don't consider myself unfit to be a mother."

"Then both of you are crazy," said Mrs. Sherwood.

That was it. Everyone started shouting and calling each other names. Mr. Taylor kept begging for calm, but no one listened. Two men started fighting and had to be pulled apart.

Mr. Taylor ended the meeting then and told everyone to go home. On the way out, the TV and newspaper reporters were all over the place, interviewing people who were eager to talk to them.

We stopped at a fast-food drive-through for sodas on the way home. We sat in the parking lot drinking them. "Why do you think people are getting so wild over this?" I asked Mom.

"I think it touches on a sensitive issue," Mom said thoughtfully. "Do you get to control your own life? Or are you supposed to do what you're told? People feel very deeply about both sides. What you think about that influences the way you run your life. When that essential belief is challenged people feel very threatened."

"No," said Mary Anne. "I don't think that's it."

"What do you think?" Mom asked.

"I think some people are just dying to know what my pajamas look like," she answered.

I pushed her on the shoulder and she

laughed. I started laughing, too. So did Mom. It felt good to laugh.

When we got home, Richard was watching the WSBK *Ten O'Clock News* with Mimi Snowden. On the screen was the meeting. "What a zoo," Richard said. "Are you guys all right?"

"We're fine," I said, sitting down to watch.

The next thing that came on was a close-up shot of Mom on a screen behind Ms. Snowden. Mom looked furious and was shouting at Mrs. Sherwood. "Tempers ran high as irate parents lashed out at one another this evening," Ms. Snowden said in her super calm voice. In the background you could hear Mom shouting but you couldn't tell what she was saying. "Mrs. Sharon Spier nearly set off a riot when she defended her daughters, who are the ringleaders of the anti-spirit movement."

"Very nice, Sharon," Richard teased Mom with a chuckle.

Mom wasn't laughing, though. "She singled me out for revenge," she said. "This is so unfair."

"You nearly set off a riot," Richard continued. "I'm impressed."

Just then, the phone rang. I went into the kitchen to answer it. At first, no one said anything, but I could hear breathing. "Who is this?" I demanded.

"Go back to California, freak," came a boy's muffled voice. "Go back or someone could get hurt."

I slammed the phone down hard.

I felt scared — not scared by the threat, but scared by the way people were acting. I thought I knew what people were like. I thought people were basically good and reasonable.

After what I'd seen and heard tonight, I was changing my mind.

CHAPTER 12

On Wednesday morning at breakfast, my eyes went right to the copy of the *Stoneybrook News* on the table. TENSIONS HIGH OVER SPIRIT MONTH blared the headline in large, bold type. In the front page photos parents shouted angrily at each other.

Mom stood at the counter drinking a cup of chamomile tea. "Front page news, two editorials, *and* the entire letters-to-the-editor section," she said.

"Wow," was all I could say.

While I sat down to read the paper, Mom switched on the radio. "Over in Howard Township," the news announcer intoned, "a man was arrested last night for intentionally running his pickup truck into the right fender of a neighbor's sports car. The incident took place outside the town hall after a meeting in which the pros and cons of Spirit Month at the local middle school were being hotly debated."

"This has got to end," Mom said wearily.

"At Stoneybrook High, the situation was equally tense," the announcer went on. He told how everyone had been shouting and fighting. And apparently someone had thrown white paint on someone else's car because of a disagreement they had had at the meeting.

"We're on local TV again," Mary Anne called from the living room. I ran to join her and saw a rebroadcast of the news from the night before.

Mom stood behind me shaking her head. "I hope no one at work saw this," she said. "I look terrible."

"No, you don't," I said honestly. "You just look mad."

"Oh, I was. I've never liked Cindy Sherwood. I've disliked her since high school."

"Are you talking about that spunky Cindy Sherwood, our old pal from high school?" asked Richard, coming down the stairs.

"Oh, you never liked her either. Stop teasing," Mom said, tossing a couch pillow at him. "Come on, we're going to be late for work."

Richard tossed the pillow back on the couch. "Do you think it's safe to go out there today?"

"Of course it is, come on."

"I don't know," Richard teased as they went out the door. "You might cause a riot. I'm nervous."

" 'Bye, girls," Mom called over her shoulder.

Mary Anne and I went into the kitchen where I poured myself some granola and opened the newspaper to the editorial page. On the left side of the paper was an editorial entitled: "A Question of Civil Liberties." On the right side, an editorial by a different writer was entitled: "What's Wrong With School Spirit, Anyway?"

The civil liberties writer agreed with Mary Anne and me. While Mary Anne ate her toast, I read her some of the editorial. " 'In a world where getting ahead often means going along with the prevailing tides, it's refreshing to see that some SMS students haven't lost touch with the spirit of integrity, personal choice, and self-rule, which are the cornerstones of our nation.' "

"Yea for us," said Mary Anne.

It seemed a little heavy-handed to me, but at least the writer agreed with us. At the end of the editorial, she suggested that the pro-spirit kids were the kind of people who insisted that everyone conform, and wanted to deny self-expression to others. Basically, she implied that if they won this thing, there was no hope for the future.

Then I read Mary Anne some of the pro-

School Spirit editorial. "What's wrong with loving your school, with wanting to see it excel? Have our children become so jaded, so filled with the vacuous TV culture around them, that they feel it's too 'uncool' to care about something as wholesome and basic as their school?" He went on to suggest that those of us who didn't want Spirit Month would grow up to be adults who felt it was "uncool" to care about anything at all. Basically, he implied that if *we* won this thing there was no hope for the future.

"He's crazy," said Mary Anne.

I skipped the letters-to-the-editor page. I didn't need to hear any more opinions just then.

"I guess we better head out to our lovely, spirited school," Mary Anne said glumly.

I nodded. "What's on today's thrilling Spirit Month agenda?"

Mary Anne checked in her folder and found the schedule. "Retro Clothing Day," she read. "Come as a student from the past."

I thought about that for a moment. "I'm coming as a student from the past — myself — Dawn Schafer on the last week of March, before this whole mess started."

"What's your costume going to be?" Mary Anne asked.

I forced a big, happy smile on my face. "This, a smile. Back then I used to smile in school."

Mary Anne laughed softly and patted my back. "Let's go."

When we reached school, about half the kids were dressed in costumes from the past. Katie Shea was wearing a long skirt, her hair pulled back in a bun. Mary Sherwood had on a sailor dress with kneesocks, her hair in ringlets. Alan Gray actually wore a toga and high-laced sandals.

I took my seat in homeroom just as the bell rang. Almost immediately, the PA system crackled on. "Good morning, students," said Mr. Taylor. "First of all, I'd like to congratulate the SMS baseball team for winning yet another baseball game yesterday afternoon. Their winning streak remains unbroken. Secondly, I would like to announce that the School Spirit Month panel has reached a decision. Effective now, School Spirit Month has been cancelled. This decision was not made lightly, and I urge all students to accept it and move on without further confrontations. Let's put the bad feelings behind us and work together as one student body again. Thank you for your cooperation."

The class sat in stunned silence. Neither side

could believe that School Spirit Month had been canceled.

I certainly couldn't. We'd won. I should have been overjoyed. Instead, I felt numb. Or maybe I was worried. Was this decision going to bring even worse trouble?

CHAPTER 13

Saturday

The DeWitts' groundbreaking party almost came to a screeching halt because the kids weren't one hundred percent happy with the way things were going. Some people are hard to please. Hey, that reminds me of some other fun-wreckers I know.

Yes, Kristy, but the Barretts and DeWitts are children. What excuse do our fun-wreckers have?

Mrs. DeWitt had asked Kristy and Jessi to arrive an hour before the groundbreaking party to take care of the kids and help get ready for the party.

Kristy was prepared to find a mess, but the house was in pretty good shape. Obviously some pre-party cleaning up had taken place. And things were calm since Jessi was already in the backyard with the kids.

"The decorations look great," said Kristy as Mrs. DeWitt led her through the kitchen and into the yard. Colorful pennants were strung along the fence and bunches of helium balloons were tied everywhere. Two long tables with red cloths were set up and a third table held stereo equipment.

"Franklin did most of it," said Mrs. DeWitt. "He's so organized."

Jessi was playing a game of mother, may I with some of the kids. She waved when she saw Kristy.

Just then, Franklin came out onto the small deck. He smiled at Kristy, then turned to Mrs. DeWitt. "Have you seen the plans I drew up for the addition?"

"I thought you left them on the living room end table."

"I did, but now they're not there."

"They've got to be around somewhere," said Mrs. DeWitt.

"Where are Buddy and Lindsey?" Kristy asked.

"Also around somewhere," Mrs. DeWitt replied. "Could you find them and ask them to help me put the food on the tables?"

"Sure," Kristy agreed. First she went upstairs. The second floor had returned to its former messy state. The toys which had been so carefully put away on Saturday had found their way back onto the floor. She picked her way over everything, but didn't see Buddy and Lindsey. She finally found them in the basement in Buddy's and Taylor's room.

Lindsey and Buddy were sitting on the floor studying some papers spread out in front of them. Kristy sat cross-legged beside them and saw that they were looking at the plans Mr. DeWitt had drawn up for the addition.

"Your father is looking for those," Kristy told them. "You better return them, fast."

Buddy gathered up the prints and ran upstairs with them.

"You must be happy that you're not moving," Kristy said to Lindsey.

"Yeah," Lindsey replied with less enthusiasm than Kristy expected.

"And you'll have more space once the addition is finished," Kristy added.

"Uh-huh."

Kristy was puzzled. She thought the kids would be thrilled. "We're needed upstairs to help with the party," she told Lindsey. "Come on."

They climbed the stairs to the kitchen, and found that Mrs. DeWitt had already put Buddy to work carrying food out to the tables in the backyard. A large glass bowl of potato salad was in his arms. "Everything in the refrigerator with the green plastic wrap goes on the first table," Mrs. DeWitt told Kristy. "The food in clear wrap goes on the second table so it will be nearer to the barbecue grill." She must have noticed how impressed Kristy looked because she added, "The color coding is Franklin's system."

Kristy handed Lindsey a green-wrapped bowl of macaroni salad and carried out a bowl of fruit salad herself.

"Are you excited about the addition?" Kristy asked Buddy as they walked outside.

"Sort of," he replied. "I guess."

Kristy frowned. This was what the kids had wanted. Didn't they want it anymore?

In an hour everything was set up. The Pike family was the first to arrive. Kristy greeted Mallory coolly. So did Jessi. Mallory wasn't happy to see them, either, and she wasn't thrilled about having to help take care of her brothers and sisters.

Once the Pikes were in the yard, Mr. DeWitt turned on the outdoor stereo and the party officially began. The adults stood and talked while Mallory and Jessi started a game of hide-and-seek with the kids. Although Mal and Jessi weren't smiling at one another, Kristy noticed that they *were* working together. She figured that pretty soon they'd be friends again. But she told me later that she wondered if she'd ever feel friendly toward Mary Anne, Mallory, and me again.

In the next half hour the rest of the guests arrived. There were a lot of people Kristy didn't know. And a lot, such as the Braddocks, the Hills, the Hobarts, and the Newtons, she did know. And even though the parents were supposed to be looking after their own kids, when they saw Mallory, Jessi, and Kristy, they sent the kids over to them.

"We should have found a way to charge for this," Kristy muttered to Jessi as she organized a game of duck, duck, goose for the kids. "It's not exactly fair."

"I know," Jessi agreed. "But what can we do? It's just for two more hours."

In another half hour, Mr. DeWitt shut off the stereo. "Since this is a groundbreaking party," he announced, "we'd better break some ground." He picked up one of two shovels that were leaning against the house and handed the other to Mrs. DeWitt. "My lovely wife and I will now dig the first dirt — and then we'll let the construction crew do the rest starting first thing Monday morning."

Together, Mr. and Mrs. DeWitt lifted their shovels over their heads, each preparing to lift out a shovelful of dirt.

"No!" Buddy shouted. "Stop!"

Everyone turned to look at him as he broke away from the group of kids and raced to Mr. and Mrs. DeWitt, grabbing Mrs. DeWitt's shovel.

Lindsey joined him. "We saw the plans you made," she told her father. "That's not what we want."

"What?" asked Mr. DeWitt, surprised by the outburst.

Suzi and Taylor joined Buddy and Lindsey. "I want whatever Buddy wants," Taylor said, loyal to his new big brother.

The DeWitts were aware that everyone was looking at them curiously. Mr. DeWitt turned to the party guests. "This groundbreaking has been momentarily delayed due to an unexpected family powwow," he announced.

Kristy stood nearby as the kids spoke to their parents. "Lindsey and I don't want all those bedrooms that are in your plans," Buddy explained. "We want two big rooms next to each other, one for boys and one for girls."

"That way we can all be together," Lindsey added.

That made Kristy smile. She could hardly believe these were the same kids who had loathed each other just months earlier.

"Buddy and I talked about it," Lindsey continued. "It will be more fun with two rooms."

"But what about quiet for study time?" Mrs. DeWitt asked.

"We can use the girls' old room for a quiet study room," said Buddy. "That was my idea. And we can use the basement as a play area."

Mr. and Mrs. DeWitt looked at one another. "I suppose we could do that and still build a small room for Marnie and one for Ryan," said Mr. DeWitt.

"By the time they're ready to move into the big room, Buddy and Lindsey might want rooms of their own. We could make a switch then," said Mrs. DeWitt. "It might work out very well."

"Sounds okay to me," Mr. DeWitt agreed. "All right, kids, you've got it."

"Only, don't change one thing," said Lindsey. "Keep the two extra bathrooms. Definitely."

"Add a bazillion bathrooms," said Suzi. "Every time I have to go someone's in there already. I can't stand it!"

Mrs. DeWitt laughed. "A bazillion bathrooms sounds good to me, too."

Suzi smiled. "See, Mommy. You won't have to lose your mind anymore."

CHAPTER 14

Whial Kristy, Mallory, and Jessi were at the DeWitts' party, I was in my room, stretched across my bed, staring at my science book. I was supposed to be reading a chapter on electromagnetic fields, but I was thinking about School Spirit Month.

After the announcement on Wednesday canceling Spirit Month, I worried that pro-spirit kids would be so angry they'd do all sorts of mean things. I also worried that the anti-spirit kids would be obnoxious about their victory and make the pro-spirit kids feel even worse.

Neither of those things happened. Instead, the spirit just seemed to fizzle out of SMS completely.

The worst thing the pro-spirit kids did was glare angrily at the anti-spirit kids. The anti-spirit kids just seemed depressed and tired out.

That was how I felt, too.

But why?

Was it because I felt bad about depriving the pro-spirit kids of their fun? Maybe. When your victory makes someone else miserable, it's hard to feel good about it.

Yet isn't that what competition is about? If someone wins, then someone else has to lose. And no one likes to lose.

Did it have to be that way, though?

I was thinking about these things when I heard the doorbell ring downstairs. "Mary Anne, Logan is here," Mom called up the stairs.

I heard Mary Anne leave her room and run downstairs. I tried to force myself to concentrate on my science book. For a few pages, I managed, but then my mind wandered again. I decided to go downstairs and get something to eat.

I heard Logan and Mary Anne talking in the living room. "Of course I care about the baseball team," Mary Anne said.

"Well, it doesn't seem that way," Logan muttered.

"Not wanting to do every single Spirit Month event and not caring about the baseball team aren't the same."

"But School Spirit Month was supposed to be about supporting the team. Everyone seemed to forget about that, including you."

I couldn't keep quiet any longer. "Logan, that is so unfair," I said, entering the living room.

"What's unfair is canceling School Spirit Month," Logan countered. "Our team worked really hard this season and we deserved the support."

I didn't know how to reply to that. I saw his point. And I could see he felt hurt — betrayed, in a way — by the cancellation of Spirit Month.

"Logan, I care about anything that concerns you," said Mary Anne (which was certainly true). "I just didn't think I should have to wear pajamas to school if I didn't want to. That's how it started, and somehow the whole thing blew up into something bigger than it should have been."

"I know."

"I don't understand why each student couldn't be free to express school spirit in his or her own way," Mary Anne added. "But, you know, I really appreciate the way you never turned on me when things got nasty. I know it couldn't have been easy for you, being on the team and all."

"Mary Anne, you know I . . ." Logan stopped himself and seemed embarrassed.

I realized it was time for me to leave and

give them some privacy. I went into the kitchen where Mom was chopping celery for the vegetable soup she was making. "Hi, sweetie," she said. "What's up?"

"Nothing much," I replied, breaking a piece of celery from the stalk. "I'm just wondering why I don't feel happier about Spirit Month being canceled."

"Sometimes you experience a letdown after a battle is won and the excitement is over," Mom suggested.

"Maybe," I agreed, but somehow I didn't think that was it.

I rinsed the celery and went back up to my room with it. I tried to read my book but it was no use. I found myself thinking about Spirit Month again.

An hour later, Mary Anne came into my room and sat at the end of my bed. "Did you settle everything with Logan?" I asked.

"I guess so. He's not mad at me, but he's still bummed out."

"You know, Mary Anne, we didn't start out wanting Spirit Month to be canceled. At first we just wanted participation to be voluntary. Then the other kids felt so threatened and got so nasty that we made our position stronger," I said. "But I've been thinking. What we did was a reaction to them. It wasn't what we really wanted."

"What are you saying?" Mary Anne asked.

"I'm saying that maybe I don't feel good about Spirit Month being canceled because it's not what I wanted in the first place."

"I haven't been feeling good about it, either," said Mary Anne. "But what can we do about it now?"

"What about another petition?"

Mary Anne covered her face with her hands. "No, I couldn't take it."

I knew how she felt.

"Then what about a proposal? We could write something up suggesting that School Spirit Month be strictly voluntary, and submit it to Mr. Taylor," I said.

"That would be all right. At least it's worth a try."

"It is worth a try," I said as I went to my desk in search of a pen and paper.

On Monday morning I found myself sitting in Mr. Taylor's office, nervously clutching the proposal Mary Anne and I had drafted over the weekend. I'd shown it to Mr. Taylor ten minutes earlier, and his response had shocked me. "Would you like to read this over the PA system?" he asked me.

"Today?" I asked, swallowing hard.

"Yes, today."

"Well, all right." As far as the other students

were concerned, I was already at the center of this thing. How much worse could it get? I had nothing to lose.

So there I was waiting for Mr. Taylor to finish his announcements. "And now Dawn Schafer will read you a proposal she submitted to me this morning. It's an interesting idea and I'd like you all to think about it." He turned to me. "Dawn."

Mr. Taylor stood up to give me his seat in front of the microphone at his desk. As I took the seat, I could imagine the pro-Spirit Month kids scowling at the idea of hearing from me again. "Hello, everyone," I said into the microphone, my voice shaky. "Here is an idea Mary Anne Spier and I have come up with."

I cleared my throat, took a deep breath, and started to read. "Spirit is a feeling. It's what's inside each of us. And what's inside can't be the same for all people. We feel things differently, and we express what we feel in different ways. With that in mind, it seems reasonable to say that while School Spirit Month was wrong for some kids, it was right for others. Some of the activities were even more suited for certain kids than others.

"What we propose is that School Spirit Month be conducted on a voluntary basis. No one should be harassed for not participating. Neither should anyone be stopped from participating. Since School Spirit Month began, there have been many misunderstandings and hurt feelings, and a lot of hostility. We propose putting that behind us and trying for a new spirit, one in which each individual is regarded as unique. We believe that it is possible to make School Spirit Month really meaningful by committing ourselves to a spirit of mutual respect."

CHAPTER 15

"Go, SMS! Go! Go! Go!" Kristy was beside me on the bleacher, screaming so loudly my ear hurt. It was the day of the big game against Howard Township, and at that moment Logan was rounding third base, heading for a home run.

The stands were packed with students, teachers, and parents, all of them going wild.

"Logan! Logan!" shouted Claudia on the other side of me.

"Safe!" the umpire shouted as Logan slid into home plate.

"Yes!" I shouted, jumping up along with everyone else. "Yes! Yes!"

Kristy hugged me hard as she jumped up and down. Claudia pounded on Mary Anne's shoulder. Mary Anne burst into tears, not because Claudia was hurting her, but because she was so happy!

"We're winning!" Mallory shouted as Jessi

jumped up and down beside her. "We're winning."

Logan had broken the tie score of six to six. The batter after Logan popped out, so it was time for Stoneybrook to take the field for the final inning. As they did, the cheerleaders led a cheer.

While that was going on, I gazed around at all the smiling faces. In just one week, the kids at SMS had become friends again. School Spirit Month was back, but on a voluntary basis. The dreaded Pajama Day came and went. Mary Anne, Mallory, and I didn't wear pajamas. Claudia, Kristy, and Jessi did. Kristy did look very funny in her bunny pajamas and bunny slippers. She stuck her hair out with gel and carried a big stuffed bunny. Claudia, of course, looked chic in her lounging pajamas. Alan Gray arrived in Batman pajamas, and three girls built a cardboard crib around themselves and came dressed as babies. It was pretty funny, and since I didn't have to participate, I was free to enjoy the silliness of it.

I did participate in the can recycling drive, and in Garden Day, both of which I thought were worthwhile. And Mary Anne even volunteered to help Claudia repair her ruined mural.

It was wonderful that the school was reunited, and even more wonderful that my friends in the BSC were back together again. (If we could straighten things out with Stacey, everything would be perfect.)

What I learned from all this was that there are always two sides to a story. And that the best solutions are the ones in which the most people get what they want.

I also learned that achieving that kind of compromise is really hard. But it's worth trying for.

The crack of a baseball bat stirred me from my thoughts. The other side had made a hit, sending the ball high and far. "Catch it! Catch it!" Kristy shouted at the SMS outfielder.

The outfielder ran backward, his mitt outstretched. The ball was still high over his head.

The Howard player was nearing third base.

If the SMS outfielder missed the ball, the Howard player would probably make it home. The score would be tied again.

The SMS outfielder caught the ball.

The Howard player was out.

Everyone jumped to their feet, screaming.

Me, too. I was excited that the SMS baseball team's work was paying off. I was proud of my school for having such a great team. I guess you could say I was filled with School Spirit.

About the Author

ANN M. MARTIN did *a lot* of baby-sitting when she was growing up in Princeton, New Jersey. She is a former editor of books for children, and was graduated from Smith College.

Ms. Martin lives in New York City with her cats, Mouse and Rosie. She likes ice cream and *I Love Lucy*; and she hates to cook.

Ann Martin's Apple Paperbacks include *Yours Turly, Shirley*; *Ten Kids, No Pets*; *With You and Without You*; *Bummer Summer*; and all the other books in the Baby-sitters Club series.

Look for #85

CLAUDIA KISHI LIVE FROM WSTO!

I flicked on my clock radio. It was tuned, as always, to the local radio station, WSTO. Some old rock tune was playing, and I listened to the end of it. My eyes started feeling heavy. I could feel myself dozing off.

"And that was U4Me — rockin' it for you here on WSTO!" chirped this goony-sounding deejay. "We've got more music for you in a minute, but first let me tell you about our cooooool connnntessssssst. . . ."

Those last two words were full of echo or reverb or whatever they call that. It was giving me a headache. I reached out to turn the radio off.

". . . Say, kids, if you've been listening to me and thinking, 'Hey, I could do that,' well, here's your chance. *You* can be the host of your own show on WSTO. That's right. If you're between the ages of twelve and fourteen — that's *years*, ha ha — you can have your own one-hour radio show, twice a week for . . . a fuuullll monnnnnth!''

My hand froze.

"You find the guests," he went on. "You plan and emcee the show. It's all up to you — if you're the winner of our Host of the Month Contest! To enter, just tell us why we should hire you — on one sheet of paper, please! Make it serious, make it funny, make it *you*! The best entry wins, and the contest ends a week from today, so hurry. And now, more *greaaaat muuuusic!*"

My mind was in warp speed.

My very own radio show? Me, Claudia Kishi, a deejay?

Yes. I could see it.

This was it.

This — *this* was what I was looking for!

**Read all the books
about Dawn
in the Baby-sitters Club series
by Ann M. Martin**

Create Your Own Mystery Stories!

THE BABY-SITTERS CLUB®

MYSTERY GAME !

WHO: Boyfriend

WHAT: Phone Call

WHY: Romance

WHERE: Dance

Use the special Mystery Case card to pick WHO did it, WHAT was involved, WHY it happened and WHERE it happened. Then dial secret words on your Mystery Wheels to add to the story! Travel around the special Stoneybrook map gameboard to uncover your friends' secret word clues! Finish four baby-sitting jobs and find out all the words to win. Then have everyone join in to tell the story!